Kelly Simmons

Based in Philadelphia, where she lives with her husband and three children, Kelly Simmons works in communications. *Skylight* is her first novel.

Skylight

Kelly Simmons

JOHN MURRAY

First published in Great Britain in 2008 by John Murray (Publishers)
An Hachette Livre UK company

1

First published in paperback in 2008

A CIP catalogue record for this title is available from the British Library

ISBN 978-0-7195-2352-6

Typeset in ITC Legacy Serif Book by Servis Filmsetting Ltd, Stockport

Printed and bound by Clays Ltd, St Ives plc

John Murray policy is to use papers that are natural, renewable and
recyclable products and made from wood grown in sustainable forests. The
logging and manufacturing processes are expected to conform to the
environmental regulations of the country of origin.

John Murray (Publishers)
338 Euston Road
London NW1 3BH

www.johnmurray.co.uk

For Dr Mittl

SUNDAY

Racine, 1977

A Polaroid with white edges. My Easter dress is robin's egg blue; it ripples against the church's red door like a flag. My father said it made my eyes look turquoise. He's not in the frame, but I know he's still alive and in front of me, taking the picture; not because I remember, but because the sky is dark and the March wind is whipping my long hair against my lips, bending the saplings next to the church, and yet I still look so completely, utterly, unafraid.

In all things, I blame the husband.

Women who sleep with teenage boys, women who shoplift collectibles, women who lock their children in basements. Yes. Their rotten husbands drove them to it.

My mother said this was the result of having a perfect father. A knight. A prince. A hero who made every other man look small, ruinous.

And that is why, when the kidnapper cracks open our new skylight like an oyster and slithers in, landing dripping wet in my daughter's bedroom, I don't blame the defective latch, the alarm system, or the thin bronze shell of the new tin roof. The dotted line of fault doesn't lead to my architect or contractor or engineer, whose chosen materials proved too delicate for my most paranoid calibrations. No. I know everything they could conjure or specify is no match for the muscle of conviction.

And oddly, lastly, I do not blame my intruder. And that explains everything that follows, doesn't it?

I am angrier at my flawed ambitious husband than the man who crouches among my daughter's stuffed animals, who stops to listen for a moment before he decides to snake toward her bed. I am angry before I even know the truth: of why our home, our tin roof, and why, why, Sam's favourite daughter. Who needs facts? My shaking body knows what it knows. That Sam is the one who leaves me alone at night with my anxiety attacks and my children and the thunder ripping open the sky, the lightning slashing our trees to toothpicks while the sounds of the storm cover the squeak of a criminal's ladder unfolding against my house.

I stand at the top of our stairs with the portable phone in my hand, my thumb on the button that should produce dial tone, and doesn't. Now there is no other sound but pounding heart and pouring rain. He is here, and he is smarter than I imagined.

St Catherine's Maternity Ward, 2003

Jordan's tiny eyes are shut tight inside the receiving blanket, as if she anticipated the flash. I look the way air travellers look when a bumpy flight finally lands. This is how all women feel, even after the third or fourth time. Yes. That's what Sam tells me, how he tries to comfort me. Everyone is afraid of giving birth. Everyone is afraid something will happen to their baby. But does everyone worry, Sam, that their ex-husband will be that something?

I remember the day I found out I was pregnant with her. Before I called Sam, before he brought home sparkling cider to celebrate, before he kissed me and told me how happy he was. As I left my gynaecologist's office, burdened with the news and the care of my other two children, I struggled getting them into their car seats. My hands started to shake a little as I brought the buckle ends together. Clattering. Jamie eyed them like china moving in the cabinet. Bad enough to flinch at the look of your mother's scarred hand, but not to trust its movement?

'Your hands are shaky,' she said.

I said breezily, 'Everyone looks different leaving the doctor's office than they do arriving.'

Jamie's eyes were wide but still soft. Compassionate, I thought, even at three and a half. I nodded twice for emphasis. Was this not true? Fear either evaporates or escalates. The paper examining gown crumples inside a wringing fist, or floats up, bouncy from the good news. I was not lying to her.

Mere minutes ago, she and Julia played with a doll's house across from the receptionist's desk. She hadn't heard my legs rattling the stirrups, or seen my tears as I watched the ultrasound.

Still, those enormous eyes. She knows nothing, or everything.

I clasped my hands together tightly, to stop the shaking. Behind me in the parking garage, a car idles. I glanced over my shoulder to be sure it is a stranger simply waiting for our space, and not someone I used to love about to mow us down.

'Mommy?'

'What, Jamie?' I asked.

'You're embarrassing me.'

'What a big word,' I said. 'What a big, grown-up word.'

I should have been happy. It was summer and the renovations were nearly complete. The shifting estimates, the money tussles, all behind us. In the end, I had what I wanted, my maze of hickory floors and cage of pale earth walls. But in the kitchen, my new French windows rattled in their open frames, as if they knew something foreign was already roaring across the crisp gardens and green backyards. The wind pushed through the screens and across my oiled teak island, upending the linen napkins in their silver holder.

When the wind picked up, I headed first to my windows. They were beautiful in the show house; opened wider, left less to the imagination, than any windows I'd ever seen. I kept leaving the show tour to return to the corner where they'd been installed, running my hand over the wood frames as if they were furniture. The Andersen Windows rep teased me: Back to visit your open window? Now I had them, and I couldn't close them tightly enough. As I pulled in the last latch, defending against the grassy air, two fat raindrops hit my arm. I didn't even stop to wipe them off.

I walked from room to room, battening down the hatches. I kept checking the burnished latches in my daughters' rooms upstairs, once for every peril: rain could get in, a tree limb, a stranger. Re-locking windows, re-tucking covers. Was I a mother or a warden? Jordan, my baby, was curled into her rag doll, blonde silk hair against bright red yarn. Next door, Julia's mop of curls were almost indistinguishable against our Maine coon cat, Willis. On her nightstand was a faded snapshot of our old house, the wide front porch, the hammock. It looked like a vacation cottage. I sighed with guilt; she missed it, all the old things we used to have. I made a mental note to talk to Scott, the contractor, about a tree house.

Across the hall, Jamie was asleep with her finger holding her place in her book. I slipped it out of her hand, put a Kleenex in as a bookmark, went back downstairs. I was wearing a path on the new Berber carpet, but couldn't see it yet. My footprints would appear to me later; with enough time and close attention, like the shape of things only visible from the sky.

As the storm came inland, I gathered candles, matches, flashlights, laundry to fold, old mail to open, and spread it out in the den. I sat alone on my twelve-foot suede sofa and bit my nails in front of movies I knew the endings to. I let myself worry during the commercials. Every flash and boom in the sky was an assumption: that the lightning would find whatever was metallic and brittle in me.

When my nails were gone, I folded the laundry and packed my briefcase for Monday. I'd already assembled the girls' backpacks. I wrote a note for the babysitter, Elizabeth, about picking them up from reading camp and taking them swimming. I opened mail from a week earlier. In the foot-high stack of catalogues, I pulled out the familiar blue Tiffany book. It was smaller than the others, modest considering its contents. On the back cover, a man in a grey suit with beautiful hands held a turquoise box behind his back. It was like a poem, that photo. The curve of his thumb, the stripe of his suit. I tore it off like Julia might, hanging on to a photo for dear life. I put it in my briefcase. It joined a reporter's notebook, an old award certificate from American Reporting, scraps of articles and scribbles, a few notes about a child labour story that was only in my head. So said Michael, my executive producer. *Claire*, he said, breathing it, coaxing it long past its solitary syllable, *what is it with you and children in peril? You're not in a third-world slum, you're in the suburbs. You need to learn the difference between a lead and a hunch.* But there is no difference in the shiver as it travels up your spine. How can they be told apart? Michael has never worked in a top-three market, never worked overseas like I have. He only knows one shade of evil, and I know a hundred. What I call experience he calls paranoia.

On the television, Hugh Grant carried Sandra Bullock through traffic. I couldn't find the scissors – art project? School poster? – so I opened a Neiman's package with my teeth. Inside the white tissue were three floral bathing suits for the girls and the pink silk nightgown I'd ordered to surprise Sam. Ordering from catalogues as if I believed in the vibrant possibility of that paper world.

The gown looked impossibly skimpy in my lap. What movie was I not watching when I ordered this? I slipped off my tank top and shorts and pulled it on without bothering to close the shutters. The bodice was as tight as a pair of hands. My neck-lace of baby rings nestled just above the V neck, as if pointing to where it was a size too small. But the silk brushing against my legs, across, between, was intoxicating after my cottony week. I fell into it like a hotel bed, allowing myself. My head settled in at the end of the suede couch and the storm found its rhythm, down a notch into steady rain. I slept.

They'd installed the new skylights the day before and all the dark corners of the house were flooded with light. The final touch. Sam hadn't seen it yet; he was away again, gone three or four days – I couldn't remember which – to somewhere. Golf outing, conference, convention. They all involved sport mas-querading as business. His clients' pharmaceutical names, those half-words that littered our notepads and pens, blurred together in my memory the same way the names of the luxury hotels did. He told me, but I couldn't absorb the information.

Was that a true telling? When I never really grasped where he was or who he was with? I knew all I needed to know: that someone was serving him steak and fetching him fresh towels, and I was home sorting his socks.

At 2 a.m. something hits the roof and I wake up. Shaking, I go to the kitchen and wrestle with the childproof bottle of Xanax. It's hard for me to open things; even after physical therapy, my hand still doesn't work right. The wind picks up, flinging small branches on the new tin roof above me. Bronze with flashes of green, the roof is beautiful but noisy. The price you pay, I was told too late. The squirrels thought it was a slide. The rain, a timpani. The new skylights are even louder. They treat me to a drum solo at the top of the stairs. The pill finally gets swallowed through my tears. I'm not the kind of person who can live in a noisy house.

A small but hard noise makes it way through my sniffing. Half click, half squeak. I look up, as if the answer is written on the ceiling. It comes again, and with each breath, I replace negative thoughts with positive ones. I stand at my farmhouse sink in the house that was never a farm and actually say my thoughts out loud, whispering into the new curved faucet/microphone. *People don't break into houses on nights like this. It's the storm. It's the wind. It's squirrels on the new tin roof, I repeat. Squirrels on the new tin roof.* As I say the word 'tin', something above me, bigger than me, snaps, then shatters. Not squirrels, I know in my bones. It sounds like glass, broken glass.

The portable phone blinks on the other side of the room. The tongue and groove is silent as I move to it, but my limbs rattle in their sockets. The scissors are not in their Lucite holder next to the phone base. I move past the laundry by the table in the hall, eyes scanning ahead. Where are the blue curved handles, the sharp steel points? Later, I will kick myself for the weapons I walked by: Sam's letter openers emblazoned with the names of drugs, a collection of heavy vases, a laundry room full of poisonous cleaning sprays. I turn my engagement ring and diamond wedding band backwards, into my palm, and continue up the stairs, as if I'm entering a subway at night.

On the landing, I stare into Jamie's bedroom across the jungle of stuffed animals against one wall. I smell rain, wet cotton, leather. His boots, I will think later. His damp shirt. He is silent and hidden, but I imagine he can hear me shaking in the doorway, molars like maracas in my mouth. Finally I make out the contours of his face and eyes, human skin among the plush bears and cloth clowns and nylon-lashed dolls that line Jamie's floor. A man. A man I do not know, have never loved, have never hurt. The only explanation for why I shake but manage not to faint or flee.

Of course he is there; I expected him, I heard him coming for years, each night when Sam left me alone with my obsessions. I turned every creak of wood into a footstep, every flying branch into a burglar, every click into the release of the safety. I conjured him, fear by fear, bone by bone until he showed himself. Mine.

He is younger than he was in my nightmares.

The plush zoo muffles our sharp breathing, my heart pounding. There is a man in my daughter's room. I don't dare cast my eyes in her direction, don't want to point her out to him. I feel her sleeping, hear her soft breathing, out of rhythm with his and mine. I look only at him.

It is beyond intimate: past sharing a bathroom, past putting your child's bloody finger in your mouth. He stares at me. I stare back. Fear, meet Regret. Regret, may I present Fear.

He moves, but not toward me. Holds a finger to his lips, a warning, and glides soundlessly, on cat-burglar feet, to Jamie's canopy bed.

No, I cry, but it comes out mangled and small. A croak.

He scoops her up and though she is groggy, half asleep, she

looks oddly comfortable draped in his arms. Her sweet face, still flush with dreams. Her shiny auburn hair. Sam's hair.

I drop to my knees and utter the only fearless words I have ever spoken: Take me, I say. Take me instead.

I'm ashamed to admit I wasn't completely relieved when he did.

Cavern Lake, 1979

The fish on my line was so small it had to be a minnow. But you can see it twisting, fighting like a marlin, bending the bamboo pole.

My father's feet are dangling from the dock, but his eyes are on my face, not the camera, registering the shock of what we'd just done. If you look carefully, past the green pail of worms, and the fiery promise of sun, a full day ahead of us, you can almost guess what happened next. How my father released the fish, and we watched it swim back into its future. How he stopped trying to teach me to bait a hook, and instead taught me to dive off the pier. And I suppose, if you are somewhat prescient, you might also see what happened before, as my mother lifted the Swinger camera to her eye and commented on what she saw through the viewfinder.

'The son you never had,' she said.

My purse is in the bedroom, I spit to Jamie through his fingers. He has me in a stranglehold with one arm, gently releases her with the other. Is he half tough? Back on the bed, she rubs her eyes to be sure she is seeing what she is seeing: her mother taken away in lingerie. A picture worth a thousand hours in therapy.

Those are my last words: My purse is in the bedroom. Not 'Take care of your sisters' not 'I love you.' If he kills me now, that's the deathbed utterance. Later, I'll obsess over my bad judgement. Does she even know how to use the cell phone in the zippered pocket? Is 'send' one of her spelling words?

His hand cups my mouth. One finger presses against my cheekbone, another across the indent on the side of my nose. He tastes of earth. A gardener's hand. Arborist. Botanist. Digger of shallow graves. My chin quivers beneath his knuckles. My tears slide into his grip and he squeezes harder.

I look back over my shoulder. Jamie is aglow from the nightlight. My daughter, my beautiful solemn first girl. The blue scissors sit on her desk with her reading camp homework. She has tears in her eyes, but doesn't scream, or speak, or follow. My youngest child, Jordan, a small tiger of a girl, might have leapt on his back. My middle daughter, Julia, ever vigilant, the last one to fall asleep, could have split atoms with her scream. It seems he had chosen the right one.

Halfway down the stairs, I think I hear Julia turning over and sighing in her sleep. I imagine her damp curls lifting slightly off the pillow, dreaming of our old house when one ear unwittingly picks up the steps in the hall. My heart sinks, remembering the last tuck of covers, my final breathy promise. I open my mouth and cry out against his fingers. He clamps his hand, yanks my waist. My toes grip the carpet, my heels brake and skid. No. I can't leave them alone. What was I thinking? The rug burns on my feet are the penalty for changing my mind.

He pulls me harder; too late.

Had he taken one look at me in the nightgown, glistening with sweat, chest quivering with fear, and decided I was worth more than a seven-year-old? He looked me square in the eye. Taking stock. If he thought in that moment, that split-second when we sized each other up, the light just low enough to hide my flaws, that I was sexy, shiny and precious, something of value, he was in for a surprise.

On the steps outside he duct-tapes my mouth and wrists, then pulls me alongside him. The flagstone scrapes the polish off my toes. Turning the corner by the picket fence, I smell my lilac bushes, feel my blue hydrangeas paint-brush rain on my calves. Drink up, I want to cry beneath the tape. Who the hell will water you now?

The driveway is long and steep. He drags me uphill. I let him. That seems impossible now. But I was half naked and wet and I'd bitten off the only weapons I had. The wind whips my hair against my lips, cheeks. Debris digs into my bare feet: nearly invisible shards of wood and tin, bent nails, fibreglass clippings, everything they intended to sweep up tomorrow. The car door is open at the top of the street. My welcome wagon or my hearse. The streetlight above us is dark and so is the car's interior.

He shoves me in the passenger seat. This is it, the next crime, what all my obsession and Xanax was preparation for. I am graduating.

The seat is soft and warm against my wet legs. I blink back at my own relief. I am astonished by what I think: That it is not nearly as bad as I imagined. And that for the first time in ten years of marriage, the tables are turned: Sam will not know where *I* am.

Puerto Vallarta, 2005

A cheap digital print. Blurry, as if someone pulled it out of the printer in a hurry. Sam's khaki pants are rolled up to his knees; he hoists a boxfish still on its line. You can see the strain in the muscles of his left forearm, the gold clasp of his watch, the one I gave him at our wedding. It's the first photo I see when I open the box.

As I recall, I drove him to the airport for that trip, so he wouldn't have to pay to park for a week. At the kerb he handed his bags to the Skycap, then gave me four small packages to mail from my office. 'Don't forget,' he added. I glanced at the first few addresses: Mexico City, Cancun.

'Isn't this close to where you're going?' I remembered something about a younger group of clients who wanted to surf and snorkel after the physician focus groups. A four-star dinner being catered on the beach. Sam complaining how hard it was to find good wait-staff outside the States.

'I want them to arrive after I leave.'

'Why?'

He hesitates, a blank space where another man would stutter or say 'um'.

'They're gifts – they have to be timed just right.'

'What about FedEx?'

He shook his head. 'That's only reliable in the States. And it's expensive.'

'You trust the mail?'

He shrugged, I sighed. Thrifty, even at the office. His partner, Hugh, a friend from prep school with the same hobbies, the same colour hair, even the same car as Sam, was different in at least one essential way: he blew through money. Born into more, so he spent more, I suppose. I'd seen him drop a thousand dollars on oysters at client dinners; he had corporate memberships at ten different golf clubs across the country. Said if you were going to be a player, you had to act like a player. He even belonged to two clubs that didn't admit blacks or women, and was irritated when Sam said he couldn't play rounds there, because with his luck, his wife would do a story on it.

At first I couldn't imagine Hugh putting up with Sam's penny-pinching. Pens in bulk. Furniture bought at auction. How could they get anything done waiting for overseas air fares to drop? Then I saw how he needed it: Hugh splurging on lobster for the catered dinner, and Sam expected to save on everything else.

Sam ran his hands through his hair, still longish and auburn, not a hint of grey. When the light landed just right, it shone with the same possibilities as the first night we met. But it was dark when he came home most nights. I didn't see him even when he was there.

'I trust you,' he said, and seemed to mean it. I wonder now if I trusted him back.

He kissed the girls on their foreheads, me on the cheek and vanished through the revolving door. Handsome and spinning, and then he was gone. Through the passenger window I saw the Skycap watch him go, shaking his head. I got out and handed the man five dollars.

I started to pull away from the kerb and the packages

tumbled off the seat. When I scooped them up I saw one was addressed to me. I smiled. One of Sam's little non-presents. The month before, when he went to Florida, he'd wrapped up an oak leaf with a note that said 'Hate to leaf you like this.' His way of being adorable and frugal at the same damn time.

I sighed and started the long circle back to the highway. In the rear-view mirror my daughters' three heads listed to the left, held back only by the curved edges of their car seats. I imagined Sam in the plane, banking southward.

'Can we go to the access road? Please, Mommy?'

Jamie, the oldest and most like Sam, clasped her hands together like a much smaller child, a matchstick girl, begging for food.

I had no excuses: no deadlines, no classes, no appointments, no landscapers to meet with, no plumbers to let in. They saw the softness in my eyes and knew they would win.

I nodded and turned left, took the road hugging the river, heading for a spot like the one my father had taken me to as a child. It wasn't as deserted as it used to be: developers had realized a muddy river was still a river, even if it ran past a junkyard and sat in a flight path. There was a bar and cantina there now, a deck strung with lights. A small boardwalk with shops that sold things drinkers would buy: sunglasses, trucker hats. Breath mints.

I turned right past the cantina, then an immediate left. The road turned to gravel, then dirt. Trees grew taller on both sides of us. I shifted into four-wheel drive, glad it was daylight. I'd taken the girls once at sunset and couldn't stop looking in the rear-view mirror for suspicious cars. Older makes, vans with dark windows. David's Karmann Ghia. When I pictured him finding us, it was always on a road like that, gravelly, tree-lined, deserted, but at night.

We passed a minivan and a pair of young boys walking

23

with binoculars swinging around their necks. Otherwise, we were alone. It's fine, I told myself. I parked and let the girls out of their car seats. They climbed onto the silver hood of my Land Cruiser and lay down, three in a row, the engine warming their spines, the backs of their thighs. I stood next to them. In another week, there would be mosquitoes, mud, heat, but there was nothing in our way, not then.

Together we looked up and waited for the first plane to pass over. Three came in quick succession, too close to each other. I frowned. I wondered who was in charge, imagined the air traffic control room, the flight deck, the workers eating sloppy sandwiches and laughing at dirty jokes, not paying attention.

The planes were white and red; we held out for the silver and blue one, the corporate colours of the airline Hugh and Sam always flew. We had so many frequent flier miles Sam gave them away at Christmas. The girls cheered when they saw the first plane.

'Bye, Daddy!' Jamie called.

'Can you see me, Daddy?' Little Jordan sat up and stretched her arms, the short blonde hairs glistening in the light. 'Here I am!'

I smiled despite myself. They believed their father could see them waving; who was I to set them right?

When the plane was past us, I turned to go and they begged for one more.

'We might know someone on that next one,' Julia pleaded with large eyes.

'Okay,' I said reluctantly. There was no good reason not to. That was my parenting style: all reasonable requests would be granted.

The next plane was smaller, a commuter. It swooped lower, displaying its underbelly: the landing gear, impossibly small, like a heavy woman with tiny feet, the square doors and latches, pieces and parts that could be open or closed, broken or functioning. I closed my eyes. Behind my lids, the plane broke apart like a toy. I felt my lips form the word 'stop', the technique that all my therapists advised. When you want to stop your own thoughts, you have to tell them to stop.

'Closer, closer,' my children cried. 'Faster, faster.'

'Stop, stop,' I whispered.

The wind picked up and I opened my eyes. I watched my children instead of the sky. The short light pieces in the front of their hair blew back. In its wake, in its pull.

'I wish I was on that one!' Julia yelled and I wanted to cry out, a dagger to my heart.

No, no.

Not you too.

His voice is dark, the phrases businesslike, but a slight accent warms the vowels in the centre of the words. I think of the odd phrase, romance language. He tells me I can pull off the duct tape. I wonder if he is too squeamish to do it, the same way I can't bear to rip off the girls' Band-aids. Do we have that in common? No, he's probably just smart. Doesn't want to give me another chance to bite him. I work the corners off gingerly, wincing, trying not to pull the small blonde hairs around my lips.

Don't scream, he says.

I breathe, stretch the corners of my mouth. Can I speak?

He doesn't say no. Did David send you? I say hoarsely.

He looks at me for a few seconds, then turns to his door. Something about his spare movement, the economy and silence, reminds me of the last time I was in a room with David. Stealth, I think. The things you don't see coming.

I hear an unwinding as he turns back to me, rope in his hands, scissors. That's my answer. He wraps and knots my ankles first, reaches for my right wrist, cuts the duct tape, pulls. His fingers stop on the rough skin below my pinkie finger. The thicker flesh slows him down. He looks at me but says nothing. Has he seen worse scarring in his line of work?

He pulls on the rope, cocks his head. Asks if it's too tight. Yes, I decide to say quietly. My rings are still turned around; he doesn't spin the rings on my left hand or pluck them off. He slides his finger between the rope and the softest part of my wrist. It reminds me of how I tested Rexie's dog collar before she ran away. He pulls his finger out, does the same on my right wrist. Same outcome. He does not loosen the rope. There are tests for everything. Some of us shake formula on to the inside of our wrists, blow on hot pizza. Others pull on handcuffs, buy extra duct tape, put chairs under doors. He wants me to believe my comfort counts. The brainwashing, the first lie.

I mistake it for softness.

Look, I need to call their babysitter, my mother-in-law, someone—

The childproof lock snaps, and I jump.

Please?

No.

I've taught my daughters to do anything to avoid a stranger's car: kick, bite, scream. I've done none of those things. I've asked nicely, but he is clearly not falling for politeness and charm; I will have to think my way out.

My eyes skitter across the seats, front and back. There is nothing weapon-like on them. In the movies there are always bottles to grab, hot cigarettes lighters to wield. This car is empty. He looks at me taking inventory. I glance at the glove compartment; it's probably locked. My toes curl into ooze: mud, only mud, at my feet. I hope it is mud, and not something worse. I hope I am not bleeding. If he doesn't kill me, I could die of lockjaw.

My mouth feels funny already. I think about tetanus shots, gunshots, pain. Stabbing, hanging, war, famine, flood. My brain edits them together in quick cuts, like a music video of death. Then the shaking comes.

I have a blanket in the back, he replies to my chattering teeth. Of course he would have this in the trunk: blankets, garbage bags, tape, rope. There is likely a shovel and axe there too. *His hands smelled of earth*. I think of the trunk open, picture the contents. Still life of death.

Tears run down my cheeks. In between my body shaking, I shake my head no.

He turns on the car and slides the heating control from blue to red. The heater blows hot and dusty on my legs, but my body still shakes. He shifts out of park.

Would you please, I sniffle, call my mother-in-law?

Pause.

Then will you at least tell me if you're working fo—

I don't know any David, he says smoothly.

Maybe he's using his middle name? Jonathan?

He pulls out into the street and the momentum brings an object rolling across my right pinkie toe.

I flinch. Something's on my feet, I say.

He leans over, rooting with his right hand, driving with his left. He pulls something up and tosses it on to his side of the dash as if he knew what it was. From where I sit, it looks like a statue, yellowed ivory. The Virgin Mary?

Are you Catholic? I blurt out.

Why? he says coolly. Do you want me to pray for you?

I look back at the dark house: nightlights glow pale green inside three windows. As we pull further away, they look as small as fireflies. Do I say a prayer, ask God for what I was owed? Protect my daughters in their beds, keep them safe? Yes. But after I mouth the words, something else sweeps across my heart: a hobo's relief. Off in the night carrying only your wits. This may be an indication of how badly I need a vacation.

I swallow hard, go back to thinking, to who and why. A journalist again. David has a motive. I am the what, now is the when. I list what I know: a Cutlass, velour interior, at least fifteen years old. Was I right to fear the older cars? He looks Latin and is about my height. He may or may not be Catholic. I stare at his hands and wrists, arms flexing on the wheel. No tattoos or distinguishing marks. Like me, he could be anybody. He doesn't look familiar.

29

Why? Is he just someone random, someone who wants money? There have been hundreds of men in my house with their muddy boots, crumpled work gloves, sawdusty hair. Some arrive at dawn; the subcontractors, closer to ten. They have seen the ten-thousand-dollar appliances. They installed the bathtub that cost more than their trucks. Each day I come home to their evidence – the coffee cups, cigarette butts, sticky bakery papers from their doughnuts. Their DNA, crumpled underfoot. They have held my keys, opened my door, refrigerator and mailbox, left their soft drinks and their handwritten bills, stained with varnish and glue from the job. I remember most of them, not all. The window guy was the only one I worried about. But none of them looks like him. Him, I would remember. Two nights before, at midnight, a car drove down our driveway and I heard something bang against the construction dumpster. I ran outside with a flashlight, fearing they'd dumped a body, a baby, a limb. Sitting on top of the pile of wood and fibreglass, shining in the dark night, was a microwave without a door. Michael's voice burned in my ear: *A hunch, not a lead.* But hunches can lead you, too. Hunches can save you.

Who? I think of Jamie still in her bed, the description I didn't have to give of the freckle on her ring finger, the small scar on her chin. A framed school photo I could have handed the police, the one with the clenched smile, a stranger's version of her.

Do my daughters know what I look like? I imagine the police asking for a description, and them going to the box of sixty-four crayons, pulling out 'Wheat', drawing me. Choosing a darker colour for my scarred hand. Jordan, asking me last year as I winced doing the dishes: Will it always hurt, Mommy? Will it ever go away?

They'll find my cell phone, I tell myself. They will. *My feet are just muddy, not bloody.* My lips all but move with the sentences. I replace worst-case-scenario thinking with best-case.

It's quiet on the turnpike. There is only a small parade of oddballs who travel in the middle of the night. We are joining the broke, the desperate, the hopped-up on caffeine.

A few trucks, one other car approach. At the first roar of their passing, I raise my bound wrists up in the darkness, wave them.

He snatches them like a man snares a fly in the air. They go down easily, quickly out-muscled, doll-like in their sockets.

Do that again, he threatens, and you go in the trunk.

Where. I swallow hard. Is this a standard threat, or does he know about me? Has he been in an elevator with me when it clanks to a stop? At Josh's surprise party last year, the host asked us to hide in a closet; I struggled to find air amidst the dark wool coats, bit my lip until it cracked. I think of the trunk closing, the line of light going then gone, and then the click. The final metallic click. Like a gun safety.

No, I cry, head shaking. Don't put me in the trunk!

Don't make me then, he replies.

There is no more warmth on the velour seats. There is not enough strength in the armour of my body. I see thin finger-nail, small bones, skull, palate. Visions of tissue parade through my head. No sugarplums, no soft sheep. I pick the hard world apart.

This is obsession, counting the haystack. There is enough to go for ever. I cover my eyes. If it has to end, I have to end it. Stop, I whisper. I pinch the fleshy part of my left hand until it hurts. Stop, I say again. It is like learning to crash-land a plane.

What?

Nothing, I say, and embrace it. Nothing.

A few minutes pass, and I do nothing, do not make him do anything.

Could you do me a favour? I whisper finally. Could you just tell me—

No.

I pause. No you're not, or no you won't?

No, I won't.

I close my mouth tightly, will myself not to open it and ask again. It doesn't matter, I tell myself.

Why didn't you come upstairs sooner? He asks after a few minutes.

What?

Didn't you hear me walking on that damn roof?

I thought you were a squirrel, I say.

He turns back to the road. A car filled with teenagers passes us slowly. The girl in the passenger seat smiles at us through the glass. I lean back to face her and mouth the word 'help'. She screws up her face. I can almost hear her say, Huh? Like, what? Then they are gone. They pass as if we are all innocent. They assume husband/wife, brother/sister. I assumed squirrel.

I breathe in and out. After half an hour or so I am calm enough to be annoyed by his roof question. I didn't exhibit the proper amount of homeowner curiosity. Was there another taunt coming: Why didn't you go to the knife drawer instead of the phone cradle? Why don't you keep your cell phone with you instead of in the bedroom? Don't you keep mace in the house? I look at him as he drives and want to start a fight. I want to say that good burglars scouted their territory, learned things: man gone, alarm disabled, tin underfoot. The moment of break-in, after all, was just a moment, a burst of decisive grace. Anyone knows all the long hard work goes before. Even *I* know that. Sam always says, It isn't a competition. But it is. I add up everything, keep score for ever, see hash marks in the air. Even when Sam and I dance, I count the number of times he steps, ever so slightly, on the tip of my toe.

Now, I have to prove myself better than a criminal? I say nothing, breathe deeply. If I start to argue with him, I might want to scream. And screaming is prohibited. Kindly refrain.

The exits on the turnpike are numbered by the miles

between them. If you are an adult who is not tied up, not on Xanax, not avoiding enclosure in the trunk, not bleeding from rusty nail wounds in your feet, it is simple to do the math. But you have to know where you started to know where you are. I don't. Facts don't live in my head, I have to go out and find them. It's one of the things Sam hates about me. What time did you leave? How much rain did we get? What temperature will it be tomorrow? The disappointment on his face when I say I don't know. When I used to take jobs in Europe or the Middle East, I'd pursue my own stories so intently I had no idea what was going on around me. I'd wake up to flooding or a sandstorm and have to call the front desk and ask what the hell was happening. So busy looking that I couldn't see anything coming.

The exit sign marked '36' is green and wet ahead of us. I've passed it dozens of times heading north on a long vacation, but never taken it. Hilly, leafy and remote, it could lead to luxury or misery, depending on who has discovered it: white trash Columbus, or old-money Magellan. We are several hours from home, I guess, no more.

He turns on his blinker, and I imbue the act with meaning: a less civilized criminal, surely, would just have swerved. The cloverleaf curves all the way around, counter-clockwise. I'm leaning in his direction. The edges of the tyres squeal, and I have something new to consume me: the possibility of a blow-out.

Your husband is gone a lot, he says.

My cheeks burn. Salt in wound. Sam goes, I stay. I bite my tongue, wish for the duct tape back.

Four nights last week, he adds. Alcohol on the fire.

Okay, so he has done his homework. But how hard was it? Couldn't anyone watching me know? Count cars in the driveway, watch Sam's golf magazines pile up on the marble counter, see one person picking up twigs after the storm. I had five laundry baskets, six garbage cans, three daughters, two hands. I carried in dry cleaning, rotisserie chickens, and false cheerfulness at dinner-time. I doled out father-tickles the girls needed at night. And I wonder: Couldn't any thief, kidnapper or murderer watching me juggle the mail, the groceries and a briefcase as I wipe the cat's feet and pour juice into sippy cups recognize me as a woman whose husband was gone? That was the kind of zoom-lens enhancement the FBI needed: *Look, there, go in tight, see that, Lieutenant? That woman is about to detonate all over her recyclables!*

What do you want from me? I hiss.

What do *I* want? From you? His small nostrils flare and he turns to me for a second, forgetting the road.

This isn't about me. Or you, or your . . . little family.

Don't I deserve an expl—

No! I owe you nothing!

I start to cry, trying not to sob, which could be interpreted as a scream. I raise my hands to my nose, but not too high; they could put me in the trunk. I feel his eyes on my tears. Now he has given me something to cry about.

Don't, he says finally.

What's the matter? Have the other women you abducted cried too?

There ha—

I look up sharply and he stops speaking. It is too late. I heard him. We are each other's first.

I lift my bound hands and wipe my nose and cheeks. He watches me but offers nothing. What can he do? This is not my car, with Kleenexes in the front visor and napkins in the back pocket. He has the things he needs, not the things crying women do.

He pulls to the shoulder, along a grove of trees. Murderers always choose trees. Old car, night, trees. But he just looks at me. It has been a long time, but I know what it means when a man watches you cry. He is waiting, afraid to ask, but wanting to be told. I tell.

My daughters are alone in the house, I sniffle. We are out of cereal and milk.

You have a pantry, he replies.

It's an odd word to hear on a man's tongue. The first thing I think. And later, much later, *How does he know I have a pantry*?

I consider my pantry and the layout of food. The granola bars are on the highest shelf, along with the bread. My own kitchen is laid out to ensure my children's starvation. Was there anything they could reach besides cans? Jamie was the tallest, at seven. Julia was five, Jordan nearly four. Water bottles? Juice boxes under the sink? Why didn't I read *Family Circle*, allow someone to tell me not just what to keep out of children's reach, but what to *keep in*? I imagine the three of them, downstairs now, socks on wood floor, slipping, climbing, no parent, no phone, no food. The heavy silver doors of the Sub-Zero refrigerator taunting them. I've always told them not to scream in the house, to save their screams for emergencies. Will they scream now? Will they run bellowing through the yards of the neighbours we hardly know?

They are babies, alone in a house, I cry. They don't have a phone, they don't know the neighbours, they don't know how to cook. You have to let me make a phone call! Begging, already. No shame.

They'll be fine.

Please call my mother-in-law and tell her to come get them, I repeat. Call from a pay phone.

In every other country in the world, children make their own sandwiches, he says to the window.

I shake my head. I see the knives, the glass jars, the difficulty of packaging. I am losing the argument, but I know I am right.

Americans are careful with our children, I sniff.

Americans spoil their children. They grow up dependent on their own comfort. And they will do anything to attain it.

That's not true.

Isn't it? How long will your daughters let their stomachs growl before they search the cupboards? A minute? Two?

A minute? My husband won't be home for *three days*.

Your husband will be home in the morning.

What?

He'll be home in the morning.

He says it with certainty. He knew Sam was gone, knew which daughter slept where.

What else does he know?

That question sends a different wave of panic along my spine. The unusual answers to my lost password questions? My mother and father's hidden names? No. It is not possible. There are some secrets Sam and I still trust to each other.

No, he'll be home Wednesday. I have his itinerary, I say stupidly.

I have his wife, he says, and pulls back on to the slick highway, tyres spinning, flying for a moment, before we reconnect with the road.

Ally's Garden Party, 1995

A party Polaroid, barely in focus. I am on the left, but Sam
dominates the frame, sitting on a low stone wall, white
lanterns in leafy trees just above his head. Ally said she
snapped the picture because she'd never seen me swooning
before. This had to be a lie; I'd been swooning my whole life.
I'd swooned in thirty-five states, in Europe, South Africa, the
Middle East. I was dizzy from it, falling in and out of men's
lives, becoming their brief story. A freelance journalist and a
freelance lover. This picture said it all: if I wasn't careful, I was
in danger of becoming a blur.

We liked to tell friends we fell in love with each other's hair.
I loved his because it was longer than it should have been; a
rebellious mop on top of a blue blazer. I liked that he'd built
a successful company, with clients around the world, without
succumbing to an anchorman haircut. He wasn't tall, and
that made the hair even more endearing, akin to a Shetland
pony. He loved mine because it was pale.

'It's the colour of sand,' he said that first night. He brushed
a small piece from my eye while I juggled shrimp skewer,
napkin, gin and tonic. 'And your eyes are the colour of the
sea,' he added.

'And the more he talked to me, the more he reached me,' I
sang back.

37

He returned a smile with his head cocked, a look I now know is his pretending to get it look. He probably had the Joni Mitchell album; who didn't? But I think he quoted her accidentally; he never really listened to it. It was a prop, like some of his books. There were other moves and looks debuted that night. The one-eyed squint, which made him look thirteen and mischievous. The double-eyebrow raise with slow blink, meant to communicate mock shock over something said. The left-hand rake through the right side of hair, which was a stall for time when the conversation lagged.

I didn't know, that night, that he had created himself. I thought his travels and accomplishments had made him lovely and interesting, tumbled him like a shaped stone on a beach. I picked him up, chose him, the way you choose a remarkable thing. Now there's something you don't see every day: good school, hotshot company, soft corduroys, and my favourite kind of hair. Wow, look at that hair. That's all it takes. One thing. In the end, I always fell in love with just one thing. The way David twisted his watch on his wrist, the dark hairs curling around the band. How Pierre managed to laugh with his entire face. Other women had lists in their heads, requirements for their mates. Let them hold out for their doctors, their earners, their ballroom dancers and makers of sick-bed chicken soup. They could wait for their forests; I was delighted with the trees.

And now, too late, I see their pragmatic point.

I remember Ally's introduction: 'This is my friend Claire, who works for WNBN. And this is Sam, who has the hottest public relations company on the east coast. So I guess . . . one of you reports what the other invents.'

Should I have turned and run at that very moment? I didn't. I laughed.

'A spin doctor, eh?' I said.

'The best,' Ally answered.

'Uh-huh.'

'Test me.' He smiled.

I frowned.

'Come on,' he said. 'Tell me something awful about yourself and I'll turn it around.'

Did Sam see the shadow spread across my face? Did he see a million small flaws fall from my heart, or just the one, the worst dark thing? We stood in a stream of white lies and idle gossip. It was a party; everyone expected a steady flow of innocuous secrets swirling on the flagstone patio.

'Claire steals grapes when we grocery shop,' Ally said quickly, squeezing my hand. She tried and I loved her for it. But Sam didn't hear her; his eyes didn't leave me.

With my left hand, the good one, I took a long swallow of gin and tonic, metal and glass against my tongue, lime and fizz in my nose. The combination revived me. I lifted my chin.

'I leave without saying goodbye,' I said.

'A woman of action,' he replied.

'I like that.' I nodded. 'Yes.'

After I knew him better, I would witness him turning pollution into waste management. Résumé gaps into sabbaticals. When Jamie fell off her bike the first time, he called the gash on her leg a scratch.

It seemed there was nothing he couldn't re-cast.

'You don't usually go for the shorter guys,' Ally said outside the bathroom.

I shrugged and reapplied lip balm. Tall, dark and handsome was overrated. The height and the darkness, combined, could kill you.

Out on the patio Sam clapped another man heartily on the back.

'He acts tall.' I smiled.

Looking deeper into the photo I see what Ally meant. That swoon is present in my face, the curve of my body. My eyes tuned to the channel that presents the world in soft filter, all dappled light. The Sam channel. I don't think I'm like that any more. I see the world the way it is now, the lost cold French fries beneath the car seats, limp lettuce in the crisper, weeds bursting out of the ground. The world is stained. I look at beautiful men on the downtown streets and think about them vomiting, burping, shitting. That's all there is.

Look again, more closely, and you'll see that I stand at the edge of the photo; half in, half out, always prepared to move on.

But I stay. I am glued inside a collage of soccer uniforms, Girl Scout cookies, paper plates and unmatched socks. I write and produce for a local station, I don't work around the world any more. I'm leaving town in the Cutlass for the first time since my youngest daughter was born. I write my own lead-in: It took a kidnapping for me to realize how much I needed a vacation.

My children have a hard time grasping that I travelled before they were born, and sometimes so do I. I sift through the photos of my younger self like a detective looking for clues. How did I get there? How did I let that happen?

What if they find those pictures first?

I know I have to start practising my story. But how do you tell your daughters about the hospital in another town, the red wagon that isn't in the garage, the men you loved who weren't their daddy? When they say, 'If I had been born to you then, would I still be me?' how on earth do you tell them no?

No, you would be a different person, you would have a different life. We all would. And who is to say if it would be better or worse? But different is always worse to a child.

And almost always better to an adult.

We drive on for what feels like a couple hours, but could be less. There is no clock in the car, no moon in the sky. We don't speak.

I glance at the blue flashes of information on the instrument panel: 60 mph, gas tank full, fluid levels and engine temperature normal. The Cutlass, though old, has been recently serviced. I still don't trust the tyres. The occasional spin and hydroplaning worry me. There isn't that much water on the road; we haven't been drenched by a single truck. The treads must be bald in places.

The velour seats after so many leather years take me back to when I was a young girl with an old car. It can be a lethal combination: bad steering, bad tyres, bad judgement. Using the emergency flashers more often than the turn signals. Trucks that roared too close as you wrestled with the jack. Strangers who stared too long as you begged for a jump. Sam knew I hated it, so he deals with our cars now; he spends the weekends getting oil changed, tyres rotated, carriages realigned, engines winterized, summerized. Some Saturdays he is gone the whole afternoon on car-related business. When he returns, I open my glove box and there is a fresh pad of paper, a small box of tissues, my favourite chewing gum. So my brakes don't squeal. My oil light never goes on. My inspection sticker doesn't expire while glued to my licence plate.

Are we going much further? I finally ask. It is a child's

question: Are we almost there? Because, I clear my throat, the tyres are bald.

Don't worry about the tyres, he says. A response you would give to a child.

The treads squeal as we go around a curve in the woods, and a scene unspools in my mind: car spinning, tyres with no grip, leaving the ground. We fly down a gully, twisting in the air, land upside down in a creek. I cannot escape the rising water because my hands and feet are bound. In my version he can't save me; he has a gash in his head, and I have to watch us both die.

I bury my wet eyes in my bound hands and try to cry quietly. My turned diamond indents my forehead.

The tyres aren't that old, he says.

This isn't your car, I sniff. You have no idea how old they are.

How do you know it isn't?

You drive it like someone else's. It's probably David's car.

I say it with conviction but doubt is creeping in. If David really wanted to hurt my family, would he hire a neophyte with unreliable transportation?

Relax, he says quietly.

The word frightened people always hear from the non-frightened. It doesn't provide any comfort at all, because it is not meant to comfort, it is meant to shut people up.

Well, if the tyres blow out, only one of us will be able to open the door and walk away.

You, he says evenly, are not worrying about the right things.

Well, how much further are we going on the bald tyres?

Five minutes.

Here is something they don't put on the label of the prescription bottle: you will need more than Xanax to get through a kidnapping. You'll need more than admonitions to take with plenty of water, and avoid operating heavy machinery.

Yes. You will need words of comfort.

42

You will need a warm blanket, salt on take-out fries, maybe free cable TV.

And you will need company.

Paris, 1991

Black and white, 4 x 6. I stand on a bridge over the Seine
between two tall thin dark-haired men, arms intertwined,
forming a kind of 'H'. My hair is still long, blown back by the
wind. My left hand curls around a small glass snow globe of
the Eiffel Tower, a gift that never made it to its proper home,
never sat on that dark blue desk. The morning after the photo
is taken, I will walk into a salon and cut my blonde waves into
spikes. That evening, running through a cobblestone alley
with fresh black eye, nearly knocking over a woman walking a
brown beagle, I will leave one of these men for the other. I will
consider it the worst night of my life, running from David and
leaning on someone else instead, and I will be wrong.

My friends called me the queen of walking away. There was
always another assignment, another location, another
someone, ready to rotate in. After Pakistan, when my sweat
shop story won all the awards for the BBC, I could work
anywhere I wanted to; leave one interesting place for another.
And there was always an interesting man to be found. One of
my camera operators, a woman named Siobhan, stole the
'Now Serving' sign from her deli and put it on the table
outside my bedroom. Before I was forced to hide myself, I
shared myself indiscriminately.

I didn't spend much time alone. Not truly alone. There

45

were always apartments, room-mates. Even hotels had people down the hall. And there were usually men. I was perpetually half of something. Call them bodyguards, call them pets. Call them teddy bears or sculptures or beautifully crafted, but impossible to operate and assemble toys. I called them lovers, but that was just a whistle of a word. Something to toss off and jangle, coins in my pocket. When one of them started to cling to me, or annoy me, I left him and found another one. It was as easily done as collecting firewood.

I used to marvel at my friends' complaints. There are no good men. Everyone is married. Only the assholes are left! And I would think: Open your fucking eyes. Pay attention. Their stubbly chins, their softened shirt-tails, their beer-foam moustaches and dark amber laughter are all around you. I can walk down any street and pick up the scent of their shaving cream.

'Don't wait for them to choose you, go out and choose them', I'd say. That's what I did. That I may have chosen badly or rashly or without enough information was completely beside the point. If you can't be in control over who you fuck and when, what can you be?

This is what I told myself: I believed I was in control. I didn't see that I was wasting my youth and grace, doling it out as if it would regenerate. I didn't know at twenty what I knew at forty: that powers of seduction slow to a trickle. Until one day you go into the city in a perfect-fitting pair of jeans, get your hair highlighted, and when you walk back to your car no one's head turns.

No, I didn't know I was perishable. But once I figured it out, the world conspired to move up my expiration date. It swatted at me daily with small swords – floods and heights and confined spaces and shadows and creaking floors. Things no one else saw. The pathetic world according to Claire.

It began the first night Sam was gone on business. I woke

up at 1 a.m. to thunder. I stood at the window and watched the young trees planted at the perimeter of our property bend sideways; wet and flailing, mops from hell. In my mind, I saw every tree in the development upended, the roots gnarled and angry as claws. They came at me, swinging, and I swear I felt their raw edges against my skin, the layered scrape of bark, the sharp points of twigs, their tightly coiled whorls and knots. I did the only thing I could think of doing, the only thing that occurred to me, the thing I was best at.

I left.

The steering wheel shook with my shivering; the road was barely visible through the overworked wipers. The night clerk behind the hotel desk, a boy really, cowered from my wet shaking hands, handed me the keycard with two fingers, afraid I would burst open, come flying apart in his prim flowered lobby.

I still recall the look on Sam's face when I told him. Just in from the airport, plopped in a leather chair, his garment bag a dog at his feet. Every line in his face flattened as if I'd told him I was a hermaphrodite, not that I was afraid.

'I think you should see a doctor, honey,' he said. 'I know you've had some tough times, but you have to learn to relax and to put them behind you.'

Dr Morgan was the first one I tried. 'Panic disorder,' he said calmly, not five minutes into the hour. Later in the session, he pointed out that its onset coincided with the anniversary of my father's death.

'It has nothing to do with him,' I countered. 'I loved my father.'

Dr Morgan nodded and waited.

'I loved him more than anything,' I added.

'Yes,' he said, and I was quiet for a long time.

'Perhaps,' he said after a few minutes, 'you feel your father left you alone. Maybe there was another ti—'

'I'm not alone,' I insist. 'I'm married.'

Dr Morgan looked right at me with those eyes, those waiting eyes. But I said nothing, forcing his hand. Someone had to say what I could not.

'Isn't it possible to be married and still be alone?'

A question I would never quite get around to answering. I had a bad habit of leaving therapists, too.

Exit 36 leads to Route 29, which if you follow it for a couple of rain-soaked hours, brings you to a strip of buildings that have the same name. Mid-County Pharmacy, Mid-County Pizza, Mid-County Motor Inn. Not a town, but what passes for a town. Apparently they have chosen to align themselves with the county, as opposed to the city or state. They have rejected the upper and lower part of it.

He pulls in and parks near the office of the Mid-County Motor Inn. Like the motel units, it's a redwood square, damp at the corners, dark around the nails. Worn and tired as a travelling salesman. The green lamp glowing in the window is the same colour as the trail of moss above the flimsy door. I try not to look at the dumpster off to the right.

The car idles. He doesn't turn it off. He turns and looks at me. Should he take me in or lock me in? I've had the same dilemma with toddlers and picking up dry cleaning. Which would be more problematic? Letting them come in and play with the plastic bags, or locking them in the car and risking arrest?

Our room is to my left, he says. I'm going to untie you.

He pauses and I turn to him.

I want your word that you will not move. You will not run, you will not scream.

I nod and look down. I don't want to be put in the trunk.

He lifts my chin with his thumb and I smell the earth again.

Your daughter's life depends on it, he says, an engine in his eyes.

I look down at his clothes. Thin cotton T-shirt, soaked through. Cargo pants, the signal of his youth. Is the gun in one of those enormous pockets? Yes, I decide.

Okay, I say. I sign on the dotted line. No screaming or running. My daughter's life depends on it.

We're being watched, he adds.

I remember reading in a psychology magazine that the third thing in a list, the third reason someone gives, is always the most important one. The truest one. *No running or screaming. My daughter's life depends on it. We're being watched.*

Okay, I repeat.

He turns off the Cutlass. That's how I'll come to think of it: the Cutlass. As in, the Mercedes is being serviced. Drive the Cutlass today. It's our car. He pockets the keys and tells me he's coming around to the other side.

In the two seconds it takes for him to walk around the car and open my door, I do nothing. I don't scream. I don't run. Someone is watching. Whoever it is sees me do nothing but watch him. He is thin, not big, but strong. I know the type. I should not underestimate his power.

Phase 1, 2005

A bad picture, but the only one Sam and I have of the
moment it truly all began. The grass is brown, defeated by
truck tyres and work boots. Above it, the late sun burns into
the raw yellow frame. We built everything around that view. I
wanted sunset outside every window; a reminder of that last
evening with David and Jesse, when the last bits of melony
light made even our sad hotel pool shimmer. A reminder to
take a picture before the light is gone.

When the renovations started, I tried to keep the girls out
of the house, away from the parade of bent nails and
sawdust, concrete and mud, and the flotilla of strange men.
Their shirtless sawing. Their loud radios. Their locker-room
jokes. They were always unfailingly polite to me, but I'd been
warned by Ally and Carrie, who'd already redone their
kitchens: Carrie came home for lunch one day and found the
carpenters watching *Real Sex* on her big-screen TV.

'Did you fire them?' I asked.

'Of course not,' she said. 'The cabinets looked fantastic.'

I scheduled art classes, dance lessons, gymnastics. But
Jamie, obsessed with animals, wanted riding lessons. We
found a stable with outdoor and indoor riding rings ten miles
away, tucked in the back of an old estate. The property was
both casual and grand: stone walls, colonial barns, a slate

51

patio where the parents watched and occasionally called out commands. 'Watch your heels, Blake!' 'Sloane, keep your reins down!' I grew up on a lake, not a farm, and knew nothing about horses, could offer no stylistic advice. Stay on, I wanted to say. Do not fall. Cling.

The mud and the hay and the barn cats kept Julia and Jordan amused while Jamie learned to tack up Hor-Hay, clean his saddle, and figure out which of his stallmates to pet and which to avoid. I was amazed by the gear: the rows of saddles and bridles, the bits and brushes and leads. The barn was like a ship, and cleaner than our garage or basement. It smelled not of swallows and manure, but saddle soap and hay.

The girls who helped in the barn were adolescent and silent: they saved their words for the horses. They had tangled hair and hundred-dollar breeches; shovelled manure in the afternoons and went home to bedrooms straightened by housekeepers. One afternoon I was surprised to see a boy in the barn; older than the others: eighteen, I guessed. He lingered over Jamie, slowly explaining things she already knew, endlessly adjusting her saddle and stirrups. Ben, his name was. He had pretty eyes and dirty fingernails.

One Wednesday, after Jamie's fourth lesson, a car followed us down the long curving drive. It was fall and the sycamores lining the gravel path were heavy with dull red leaves, and in the rear-view mirror looked like they could fall on either car at any moment. My route home was winding and circuitous, but the other car, an old green Mercedes, stayed behind me. I was two streets from our turnoff when I turned abruptly, without a signal, on to a dead-end road. The Mercedes kept going straight.

'Mom, this isn't our street,' Jordan said.

I turned around slowly, pulled back on to the main road, and looked for the green flash of the other car in either direction. Gone.

'Do you know what kind of car Ben drives?' I asked Jamie.

'He rides his horse to the stable,' she said. Then added, 'Don't be paranoid, Mom.'

I pulled out and kept driving. I repeated the phrase 'late model forest-green Mercedes' over in my mind, intending to make a note when I was parked. At home another car, a brand-new SUV, was next to Sam's in the driveway. I saw two heads through the family room window, bowed over floorplans.

While the girls kicked off their boots, Sam introduced me to Roger, who stood up when I walked into the room. He held a mustard-coloured cap in front of him, running his thumbs over the clasp. He was not quite as weathered as the others.

'Roger is Scott's window guy,' Sam said. 'And Claire is my wife.'

'There must be some mistake,' I said. 'I've already ordered windows.'

The men looked at each other, confused.

'Scott knows,' I added. 'He spoke to the Andersen rep.'

'You wanted Andersens for the kitchen area, was my understanding, but there's still the rest of the addition, plus the sliders. Couple of skylights on the second floor as I recall. I work with Scott all the time. Volume pricing.'

Sam nodded approvingly, and I said all right. I was outnumbered if it involved saving money. We sat at the dining room table while the girls' pizza warmed in the oven. Sam left to get a calculator, rubbing his palms together as he walked.

'You know,' Roger said, shaking his head, 'you look really familiar to me.'

I stared at the floorplan, afraid to look up.

'People always say that,' I replied.

'Did you grow up around here?'

'No.'

'Me neither. I'm from the Cape.'

I held my breath. David's parents lived there. I looked up, finally, and tried to measure him as he would a window frame. Blue eyes. Tan face. Hair the same colour as mine. Could he tell me what I want to know? Or would he be the one to tell David?

'Where'd you go to school?'

'Out West.'

'Hmm. What's your maiden name?'

'I just have one of those faces. Really.'

He shook his head vigorously. 'Oh, it'll probably come to me in the middle of the night.'

'Right,' I said.

Before he left I asked him for his card. Roger Berenson. I shoved it in my pocket to give to the private investigator, along with my note about the Mercedes. It had been a year since I had anything to go on, but still.

'So my crew will be out to install in a couple weeks.'

'Not you?'

'Oh, I'll supervise. I'll be in and out. I hand-pick my own guys – lot of old salts and a few Mexicans. Good ones, though.'

I smiled and thought of Carrie's story; as long as they kept the television off and did their work, I didn't much care what colour they were.

After he left I made a salad, and Julia asked Sam if we could have a horse.

'Not this year,' he said. 'But next year, you can start lessons.'

'Oh, goody! When I'm in first grade, I can ride Hey Whore!'

Sam and I burst out laughing, and Jamie corrected her: 'It's Hor-Hay,' she said.

'She always gets that wrong.' I giggled.

'Her mother's daughter,' Sam said, smiling, and started to clear.

When we put the girls to bed, I told Sam about Roger's questions.

'I'll take care of the windows from here on,' he said. 'Don't worry about Roger.'

Room 7. Gold key with a green plastic tag. He already had it in his cargo pocket, along with the imagined gun. I never figured on the key. Did I suppose he would sign us in as a couple, write Bonnie and Clyde in the registry? Of course he had the key. There was something else he needed in the office; he wasn't gone that long. He hadn't prepared for my tin roof, but that was his only misstep. So I thought. He has two deep pockets on each side of his pants. He could have anything inside them. At the school my girls attend, the principal sent home a note: no cargo pockets. Apparently boys were smuggling in iPods and Game Boys. Suburban contraband.

He opens the door to double beds. I take the one nearest the door. (Better for escape.) The bedspread's stripes are nubby beneath my bare legs. If I stayed there long enough, it would leave an imprint on me.

I look around: nothing in the room is his. No suitcase, no shaving cream, no book on the nightstand.

How long are we staying? I ask.

Until the problems of the world are solved, he says.

My hand goes up to my neck. I haven't covered anything but local stories in a decade. Has he mistaken me for a real journalist? For the person I used to be? I remember what he said earlier, that it has nothing to do with me or my family. Nothing personal, but I'll have to kill you symbolically now.

Did you say, the world?

It's just an expression, he says. He looks half alarmed, half amused.

I blink. A foreigner explains the vagaries of the English idiom to the writer.

Where are you from?

He blinks. Mexico, he says softly.

You speak English awfully well.

I learned on the job.

The lamp between our beds is two colours of orange, glazed. I finger it, wondering who made it, where it came from – Chile? Santa Fe? – instead of determining how far it would fly before it hit his skull.

He moves my hand away from the lamp. It is time to re-tie me. He pulls a length of rope from his left pocket like a magician. I expect great things from that pocket now. I want a turkey and avocado sandwich, a compass, a bottle of Ambien.

He tests the rope again, one finger against the softest part of my wrist, the inside, away from the scar. As if he knows not to touch me there. It is completely professional, a doctor's touch. He is experienced, I see now. His moves are second nature. He uses the rope to pull me to the other bed, nearest the bathroom. Worse for escape.

You should sleep, he says.

And you? I ask.

I'll sleep when I'm dead.

I blink. The phrase brings me back a long way. What was his name again? John? No, Joe, I think. The producer I met in Turkey, who sounded like a fortune cookie. It was charming at first, and helpful, the way a book of quotations can be. Until I realized he had no phrases of his own, couldn't construct a sentence from a pile of words. He wasn't tall enough; he spoke in proverbs. Goodbye, Joe.

I stand up, try to pull down the covers with my fingers. He walks over and does it for me. I'm thankful, but don't thank him.

My head is heavy against the pillow; with Sam gone, I hadn't slept well the night before, or the night before that. I yawn and don't bother to cover my mouth with my bound hands.

He sits against the headboard of the other bed, looking out the small divide in the picture window, where the Dacron curtains don't quite meet.

In the morning will you call someone about my kids?

No answer.

I sigh and put my bound hands against my stomach. There is nowhere else for them to go; they are like Barbie hands, designed to move in only one direction.

If you won't tell me who you're working for, are you at least going to tell me why we're here?

Maybe tomorrow.

Are you going to hurt me?

Not unless I have to.

He turns off the orange lamp and it is, suddenly, completely black. I guess at the time: three thirty? Four? If it was five, it wouldn't be this dark, not even in Mid-County.

My breath catches between my teeth. It's darker than anything I've seen in a long time. Dark as that alley in Paris. Dark as the refugee camp in Turkey. I've avoided darkness for years: our house is a maze of nightlights, a series of green- and blue-lit runways anyone could follow.

The cars hum on the highway, the new tyres and the not so new. But there's no television in the room next door, no laughter, no snoring, no others near. If someone is watching, they are doing it very quietly.

My heart pounds in my ears. I imagine the very last particles of Xanax disintegrating, too small for all the places they need to go.

It's too dark, I whisper hoarsely, throat dry.

Without a word, without a sound, he rises and turns on the bathroom light, leaves the door open two inches.

One of Joe's platitudes comes back to me: Words whisper. Actions shout.

Was that his name? Joe?

MONDAY

West High School Prom, 1980

A few boys asked me, but I said yes to Luke and his blue eyes and white tux. I wore an eyelet dress for the first and last time. It was the second of three dates: he took me to a movie, to Prom, and to my father's funeral.

He stopped calling after that, and my mother tearfully told me I would never find a man who loved me as much as my father. But that didn't stop me from trying, did it?

I never noticed it before, but it's possible I started here, with Luke, and the way his face came alive when he smiled the exact same way my father's did. I saw it for the first time as he waved at Luke and me through the tinted windows of the rented limousine.

My daughters are due at summer reading camp by nine. Elizabeth will pick them up at three.

That's my first thought as I open my eyes. I blink and look around the strange room. I never sleep on my back. I go to rub my eyes and am surprised by the rope.

At eight o'clock, the girls' pink backpacks wait in the mudroom, packed with books for camp and swimsuits for later. The miniature teddy bears on their zipper pulls wait for their fingers; their embroidered names call to them. Two days after I bought them, the station did a segment on the dangers of monogrammed clothing, and how it made it easy for strangers to pretend to know your child. But I couldn't take them back.

Jamie's backpack was fuller than the others; she'd been reading a series of books about demons in odd combinations, like half hawk, half cat. She is on book number four. How will she feel about reading mysteries now that she's lived a different plot? Will the librarian look in her eyes and see the fear, see it brightly enough to steer her toward something magical and hopeful?

I worry that Elizabeth will arrive at three and not find the girls. What if it takes that long? If the camp assumes they're sick and I forgot to call?

The crack in the curtains lets in a bit of sunlight. He's not on the bed next to mine, yet the striped bedspread holds the shape of his body. If I could put my hand there, which I can't, it would be warm as the hood of a car.

The bathroom door is closed with no light trickling from beneath. Could there be a window in the bathroom? Is it light enough that he doesn't turn on the switch?

I manoeuvre to a sitting position and sniff the air for shaving cream or shampoo, the sulphur of a match, some sign he is in there doing something. The air smells so distinct that when I think of it later, it's as if it's bottled and named 'cabin in the woods': a not unpleasant combination of damp redwood, brewing coffee, dusty bedspread. Yet, none of the limes and mints of most mornings, the tang of the first person up. My heart races with the truth of it. *I am alone.*

I scoot to the edge of the bed and stand up. The pink silk nightgown is damp. It clings to my cotton underwear, and I can't reach around and pull it away. One of the little things he's taken away.

I hop to the bathroom, put my hand on the door knob. Should I? What if he is sitting on the toilet, turning the pages of a magazine? I close my eyes and turn it slowly. Push. It's hollow and light as a balsa wood airplane. It fans the air with the same sound as a twig.

I blink at the empty room. Two towels, folded. A medicine chest, thin soap wrapped in paper. Unused. He is, I realize now, either in the car, watching, or sitting outside the door, guarding.

He has discounted the window.

The square above the toilet is small. It's a bit high for a woman encumbered with rope and particularly high for a woman prone to panic attacks. Aha, I think. He *knows* I'm afraid of the window. He believes I would choose the door. I stand on the toilet, pinch and slide the silver latch, make myself as small as I can. I pull up, clinging to the frame with my fingers, grateful to my yoga teachers. My knees are against the frame, then shoot out. As I turn hands and body I manage to scrape both shins badly. Metal again, cut again. I hang bleeding against the damp redwood, my nose inches away from slimy moss, my bound ankles three or four feet above the ground. Ancient hardware connects the redwood; the steel heads have transformed into stubborn rusty barnacles. If I let go, I'll be scratched by every one before I hit the ground. As I will myself to let go, scraping be damned, I feel an arm around my waist.

He pulls me down, circles the rope on my legs with his right arm, and carries me honeymoon-style around to the front door.

He kicks open the door and swings my feet to the floor.

You know what I think? he says. I think you want to be hurt. I think you want to be put in the trunk.

No.

What then?

I hop to my bed angrily, sit down. What do you want me to say? You think I wasn't trying to save my kids, I was just getting some air?

He shakes his head, takes another length of rope from his pocket and ties my hands to the base of the bed.

Your children are fine, he says. His finger lingers on my red scar. Is this recent? he asks.

No, I say quickly, then immediately regret it. I should have said yes, gotten sympathy, looser knots, something.

He goes back outside. Something in the way he walks makes me think he is more amused by the window incident than angry.

I sit on my bed with my nightgown covering my scabby knees. It's best if I don't look at them. It was months before I could look at my own right hand. Even now, when I'm doing yoga on the occasional night Elizabeth stays late, I find myself avoiding it. When the teacher says: Look at your right hand.

67

Focus on that middle finger of your right hand, I resist. Don't make me dwell.

I comfort myself with the fact that I don't feel my knees bleeding beneath the silk. I try to divert my thoughts, but when I close my eyes I see Jordan, my baby, rubbing her eyes before bed. And then, Julia, my middle child, frightened in the night. Will she remember that I sat by her bed until she fell asleep, recall our final sleepy exchange, the promise I did not keep?

I look out the crack in the scratchy curtain. The sun is orange and rising. East, I think; maybe six thirty, maybe seven. He is leaning against the hood of the Cutlass now, with his coffee. I imagine from that precise angle he could sense me opening either the picture window or the bathroom window. The building is so old it probably shakes and groans whenever a kidnapped woman hops. He sees me looking and I look away. When he comes back in, he is carrying one open cup and one closed.

Please . . . just call my mother-in-law, I say quietly. My kids are probably awake.

I can't do that.

He unties the second rope, offers the cup with the closed lid.

I don't drink coffee, I sniff. I should have said no thank you, but my manners are tied up now.

I know, he says.

He places the warm cup in my bound hands, removes the lid for me. The teabag string dangles to one side.

I try not to look at him as I take my first sip. I take the kindness out of it; he probably learned these things by going through my garbage, or by following my family to Starbucks and rooting through the cup holder of my Land Cruiser. I imagine him opening my Thermos and finding the teabag at the bottom, a kind of treasure, damp and fragrant, still warm, a comforting shape in your hand.

Still, he remembered, and how many men had forgotten?

Had come in to the bedroom and said, I made you coffee as if it was a gift?

Thank you, I say.

I sip the hot liquid as the room fills with sun, warming everything, and am grateful for the lack of lightning, wind. There is no precipitation.

First snow, 1991

It used to be framed; you can tell because of the darkness around the edges where it was protected from light. But there is very little colour in the photo; it's almost all white. Returning from a rare walk alone, hoping David was finally awake and outside shovelling and salting, I come upon a scene so enchanting I had to take a picture of it. There is the baby in a white fleece bunting, nestled in a white bouncy seat near his father's boots, holding one hand out to the magical snowflaked sky.

'Who took this?' people used to exclaim. 'Did you know this little boy? It should be on a Hallmark Christmas card!'

I'd smile and try not to consider what the message would be inside that card: That everything you try to hold on to will melt to nothing in your hand.

One January before Jordan was born, when Julia was a month old, and Jamie had just turned two, Sam had to go to California for a week. A few inches of snow were predicted, and when I kissed him goodbye at the airport, I was worried mostly about his flight. I was not worried about a dusting of snow; snow was soft and quiet; it arrived without thunderous fanfare. Rain scared me, not snow.

After dinner I bathed the girls, one after the other, and put them to bed at the same time: seven thirty. It was satisfying to see them clean in their flannel cocoons: Jamie in her brushed pink sheets, Julia wrapped in her yellow receiving blanket. As I leaned down to turn on the nightlights that led from their rooms to mine, the sweetness of their shampoo lingered in the air.

I put myself to bed at eight, since Julia still took a 2 a.m. feeding. Out the window there was no real snow, just a few flurries, illuminated by the floodlight.

When I woke up it wasn't dark, and the baby monitor was quiet. No cooing, no rustling. She made it all night. I smiled. Above the covers my nose was cold; I kicked them off and felt immediately the lack of heat.

I looked out the window. Fifteen inches, I guessed. Fifteen inches and blowing; a power line drooped between two trees near the garage. My SUV useless on the uphill slant until the driveway was shovelled.

I made a fire and heated Julia's formula in a pan over the coals. I used my cell phone to call the neighbours: no answer. I called every snow removal service in the yellow pages. No one had an opening for days.

I wasn't supposed to exercise for a few more weeks, but I trudged up the driveway in knee-deep snow, the battery-operated monitor clipped to my belt, to see if I could flag down a snowplough. Our street was unploughed and eerily quiet, the silence only broken by an occasional tree branch protesting at the weight of the snow. A woman sped by on cross-country skis, not even looking at me.

I went back and fixed both girls lunch, and tried to get them to nap in the living room, near the fire. After an hour of fussing and fidgeting, I gave up. I slid Julia into coat and mittens and strapped her into her play seat, carrying it near the family room window that faced the driveway. I gave Jamie a book and instructed her to sit in the chair where Mommy could see her. She was not to go in the living room near the embers of the fire. No.

Outside, I could see them both easily through the window; I told myself it would be fine. They are safe. 'You can see them,' I said out loud.

I retrieved the shovel from the garage. It was two thirty; I had an hour and a half of light to tackle the wet snow. This, undeniably, was exercise. As I dug in, my arms shook and I felt the flow from my post-partum discharge surge. Was that why I wasn't supposed to exercise?

I had barely cleared the walk when I looked through the window and didn't see Jamie in the chair. Julia blinked back at me in her baby seat, offering no clues. I rushed to the door, thinking fireplace, shrieking. After one terrible second, Jamie appeared around the corner, crying that she was cold. I put down my shovel and went inside, hugged her and sobbed, the tears burning my icy cheeks. I stopped shovelling and rebuilt the fire. We had toasted marshmallows for dinner. There was wood in the garage. There were cans in the pantry. The temperature rose as the power crews worked, and by the time Sam came home a few days later, the electricity was back and almost all the snow had melted. As his cab pulled in at midnight, just a light crust of it lingered at the edge of the lawn. My footsteps through the woods had melted first, but when I looked carefully I could still see them in the flattened grey of the winter grass.

Here is how it's done: when he takes a shower, he chains me to the headboard. When I have to go to the bathroom, he unbinds my hands but not my feet. It's a necessary part of our existence together, like putting a baby in a playpen when you need to unload the dishwasher. It's just what you do. The rhythms of his movements – the knotting and tangling – carry that truth. He's not being cruel: he is doing what needs to be done. I feel how children feel about the ritual of car seats. I don't put up a fight.

Did he know that about me? That I would not fight constantly, but pick my moments?

Perhaps I am easy to read. God knows when I go back over my life in my own head, the path that led me to David and Jesse and Sam, it's not hard to see where I went wrong. I know nothing of his life, but I sense his mistakes are few. Tin roof is one. Phone is two.

He pulls the chain from his cargo pocket, another magic trick. A tool belt is superfluous when you have cargo pants. He positions my hands well away from the phone. I could never have reached it with my hands or my feet. But did he forget about the rest of my body?

I wait twenty seconds into his shower, certain he'd take a long one; men always do. I work the receiver off with my knee. Lean over and press 9-1-1 with my nose.

When the operator comes on she asks what my emergency is.

I hesitate. There were several emergencies. Which first?

The shower squeaks off.

I freeze.

What is your location?

3-6-2 Montgomery Avenue, Westtown, I whisper quickly.

I do not say Mid-County. Do not say room 7.

The bathroom door flies open. As he leaps, water spins off his skin; his towel flaps at his waist, revealing the edge of his pubic hair. He pounces on me, lunging for the phone, ripping it from the wall. His knees dig into my thighs. The weight of his entire body holds me down – stomach, legs, arms. He is larger, his muscles more angrily protruding, than I imagined. With a start, I realize I feel his scrotum, a small but heavy pouch against my silk nightgown.

He throws the phone across the room; it hits below a picture of a mountain range, knocking it off-kilter.

He sits back on his heels, on my bed. Off me but panting with effort. I am wet from his shower.

I want to rub my scraped knees, but can't. He hurt me because he had to. I feel more coming, and my hands begin to shake. Will he kill me now? Or does he still need me? I close my eyes, try to do my visualizations. *Clear blue water. Swinging hammock.* All I can visualize is a bottle of Xanax at the bottom of my purse.

He pins me back down, his hands squeezing my wrists so hard they will bruise.

Did you give them your *home* address?

I say nothing, look away.

Did you?

My bottom lip quivers and I bite it to stop.

Yes, he says with an exhale I feel on my cheek. You gave them that address, not this one. You didn't have time for two, and you chose them.

I just want my kids to be safe. I start to cry. Please don't kill me or . . . put me in the trunk.

76

He releases me and stands above me for a second. I finger my necklace, run the rings back and forth across the gold chain. The threading sound is comforting to me. He goes back to the bathroom and turns the shower on again. I twist my wrists as much as I can. I imagine he expects an occasional outburst.

His head reappears in the bathroom door.

If your husband cared as much about the safety of children, or the safety of people, as you do, we wouldn't be in this situation, he says.

What situation? What do you—

He closes the door on my question, leaves a two-inch gap. I don't hear the shower curtain slide shut this time. He is taking no chances. If the door opened on the other side, on the left near my bed, I would see him standing in the steamy room, the water breaking against his shoulders, making all his hair even darker, wet and glossy as ink.

Through the open door, I smell a familiar lather: baby shampoo.

It is the first time it has ever brought tears to anyone's eyes. My babies. I can smell the sweetness of their scalps, the salt at the edges of their eyes, the moist pocket between ear and neck. The police will go to them now. They will go and they will call my husband, my mother-in-law, the sitters, my office, all the numbers on my bulletin board. People I've met, people I love or hate or barely know, people I have completely forgotten will be asked questions, and they will say things that are smart or stupid or untrue. They will say I was quiet. Sam will tell them I liked gardening, travelling, books, old movies. What do they learn about me? Nothing. Sam won't tell. And the others don't know. Not my neighbours, the women at my health club. No.

They will say I had no enemies. No enemies that they knew of, no.

All-nighter, 2006

One of the assistants took a picture of the whole group who worked on that seven-part corruption story. Michael, my boss, is on one side of me, Josh, my favourite editor, on the other. There are three interns whose names I can't remember, probably because they did nothing but order us take-out and ask questions. Crouched in one corner is my former assistant, Janice, who quit abruptly after I asked her to work late two nights in a row. And there are two other writer/producers, Bill and Sondra. I called her Sandra for a year before someone straightened me out. I can't say that I knew anyone in the picture well except Josh.

If you forced me to add it up, I would have more enemies than friends. That's the truth of it, I'm afraid. Ally knew me the longest, and knew the most about me. Carrie I'd only known since I married Sam. My other friends from college and travelling, the cameramen, the producers and directors, we'd become holiday-card friends. On the enemy side? Not just David – all the ex-boyfriends, their mothers and sisters and friends. After a break-up, I had a childish ritual – I changed my hair. The styles were certainly all there in the box. Long or short. Blonde and blonder. I was young enough, and stupid enough, to believe I could assume a new persona. In the heartbreaker protection programme.

My work didn't always create friends, either. It was my job to dig and uncover. After Pakistan, I got hate mail from people inside the clothing companies. And then there was what Michael always said to me as I edited and re-edited my stories. 'You are your own worst enemy, Claire.' Enemy? I would wonder. Because I'm trying to make them perfect?

But as my anxiety attacks worsened, the job became harder.

Stories about corporate takeovers or disgraced politicians or suburban sprawl were easy. But death, destruction and disaster were another matter.

Once I was working late on a piece about weather predictions. We'd interviewed men all over the country who claimed they could read the fish and the tides. Editing the segment required, inevitably, stock clips of bad weather: tornadoes, tsunami. I sat in the editing suite with Josh, the child prodigy fresh out of film school, and lowered my eyes while I gave suggestions.

'Just take the best four-second piece of destruction and lay it in.'

'Maybe pulse the water incidents with one that shows wind.'

Josh knew I couldn't watch. Late nights at work revealed everyone's peccadilloes. Michael can't think without pacing. Marilyn threw up before she went on air. Claire can't watch footage of blood, disasters or wounded children. Wounded children: that was the worst. I would never forget the sight of those children in the sewing factories – their fingers bleeding and swollen, putting seams in silk dresses while they sat in cast-off rags.

Luckily there aren't stories like those in my future. I don't have to tramp through war-torn countries, report live from the devastation. As a writer/producer, I was almost totally behind the scenes, doing interviews, writing voice-over, sending cameramen out.

That night, Josh had to choose his words carefully: 'Do you want residential rubble or commercial? Tornado filmed through a car window or from a redwood deck?' But occasionally he would slip up: 'Should we go with the roof flying off the split-level or the minivan sucked away in the flood?'

And suddenly the piece re-edited in my head. I saw the children lose their parents, the parents lose their children. My hands squeezed against my eyes. Josh never turned around; he just worked the keyboard and cheerfully said, 'It's looking good in its own gruesome way. There's spring water in the mini-fridge,' he'd add, punctuated by the clicks of his fingers on the keys and dials. 'Or beer. Why don't we split a beer, Claire?' And when we won awards for our stories, as we'd done two years in a row, he'd brush aside my praise. It was your brilliant idea and crisp writing, Claire. All I did was push a few keys.

Other producers and reporters were more annoying: they leaned over Josh's console and breathed onion breath on his head. They spilled coffee on his keyboard. They yelled at him for being too slow. I freaked out, but I did it quietly. And I trusted him to make the decisions when I covered my eyes. In return, he never said anything like our anchorman Bill, who complained in the voice-over booth when he didn't know the mike was on: *'Claire shouldn't do hard news any more. Since she's had those kids she's gone soft!'* I pushed the talk-back button and said, 'What's that, Bill? Your penis has gone soft?'

Most men, when they become aware of your quirks, are mildly amused. They watch with a kind of wonder, as if they are observing a species quite unlike themselves. I've seen this look on Michael and Sam and countless others. I imagine it's how we look to fish, our faces distorted on the other side of the aquarium.

Fear doesn't always serve you in life. It lives on your surface, visible as your skin. People can take advantage of your weakness. Dogs can smell it on you, and so can children. But when you turn it outward, and fear for the lives of the world, you can warn someone. You can save someone. You can see the potential for destruction around us all. It's what makes me certain I'm a good journalist. But a very, very bad seatmate on an airplane.

Two weeks ago the sun broke through the noon clouds and I decided to go out for lunch, something I rarely do. When I came back, Josh asked me to come to the editing suite and look at something. He closed the door.

'Claire, a guy was here asking questions about you. Said he saw your name in the credits and wondered if you were the same Claire he went to high school with. Said you were an amazing writer.'

My heart thumped loudly, once, in its row of beats.

'That's odd,' I said slowly.

'He asked how old you were, if you had a scar on your hand, if Cooper was your married name.'

'What did you say?'

'I told him I had no clue.'

'Good.' I swallowed hard. 'That's good, Josh.'

'He could easily be a psycho.'

'Yes. You did the right thing.'

'He kept saying, "She's blonde, right? Just turned forty? Maybe she has a couple kids?"'

'You didn't tell him about my kids!'

'No, no, no. In fact, I told him he had the wrong Claire. That you couldn't possibly be forty.'

I smiled. God bless Josh and his low-key charm. I asked what this man looked like, as if I needed to. He tells me exactly what I expect to hear: tall. Dark hair. Muscular. Then quietly, tenderly, fearing the answer, I asked him if the man spoke to anyone else: Michael? Weaselly, loudmouth Bill? He shook his head no. He didn't think so.

'Good,' I said. 'Good.' Then I left the cool hum of Josh's room, the knobs and buttons, the screens and lights that glowed like landing gear, and went back to my desk in the newsroom.

I can just see the light in Michael's eyes as the tale unfolds, how it would obliterate the notes on the newsroom blackboard, the other things we're chasing. The delight would overtake even his disbelief over my child labour story. There is nothing like the face of a journalist when he realizes he is in the presence of a story. Does a hunter ever tire of glimpsing antlers? He would shake his head and say, 'Well, Claire, I guess this explains a few things. Not to mention ruling out running for public office.'

A joke. The shortest version of anyone's life is best told as a joke.

Then I get to the worst part, or the best part to a man like him.

He stops laughing, has to. He sees my mistake, the gamble, the failure. It would colour everything, that story.

That's why so few people know it.

As Josh leaves that night, I run after him, touching his sleeve.

'I know you would probably have mentioned this, but—'

'But what, Claire?'

'This man . . . was there a young man with him? Blond, I think? Maybe who walked with a limp?'

He looks at me, but I could see the footage running through his head; a story waiting for him to edit, to make some sense of.

'Claire, if you're in some kind of trouble, if you need help—'

I wave him off with a laugh. 'Don't be silly,' I say, and he goes home.

Forget your hunch about me, Josh, just as I will forget my hunch about boys making furniture in their father's factories. Just because it might be true doesn't make it your story.

When are we leaving? I ask when he comes out of the bathroom.

He is dry and clothed now. His pants are the same, his shirt different, and the old one is wadded like a rag in his hand. Where did he have this shirt hidden? Pale blue against his light brown skin is a flattering combination. I have nothing new to look at, so I stare at his chest.

We aren't, he replies.

The ends of his hair curl up and he rubs them down with a towel. He walks over to the broken phone and takes a screwdriver out of his cargo pocket, clicking and grinding the metal against metal. He dangles something the size of a razor blade in front of me, then puts it in his pocket.

Caller ID block, he says.

I wasn't on the line long enough to trace the call, if they even have such equipment in the middle of a county. We both know this. But he wants me to know he has it covered.

The show of ripping the phone out of the wall, of pinning my arms, was that just a show? So I would know what he was capable of, even if he didn't know what I was? I try to decide if he looks harder and meaner now, in his clean blue shirt.

He goes back into the bathroom. Water running. Heavy. Too loud for the sink. I hear a squeaking sound I would know anywhere, in any county, in any bathroom. A white rubber stopper, a small chain. Water, bath.

He comes out and unties my wrists. He is close enough for

me to reach around his neck and squeeze. I don't. Perhaps his show has had the desired effect. I look away from his baby-shampooed hair, his temporary freshness, his minty teeth. He lifts up my feet. The rope is tighter there, rubbing my ankles raw. I'm aware of the stubble on my legs as he works the knot back and forth. The rope hurts and I bite my lip. This is my show; he will think me tough now.

He leads me by the wrist to the door. Two people, hand in hand, who don't know each other.

There are bubbles in the tub. I turn to him slightly and he drops my arm.

I guess you're not drowning me, then?

Five minutes. He smiles.

He turns off the spigots, leaves the door ajar.

I yank off the nightgown that doesn't fit, that isn't me, that will never have the intended effect. I slide into bubbles and don't care that he can hear them as they pop. My back squeaks against the cold porcelain and I laugh. There is a rusty spot near the faucet that would have bothered me yesterday, doesn't now.

The number of things to be afraid of is dwindling.

Yesterday I was alone. Today I'm not.

I remember the second doctor, Dr Kearny: You are afraid of being alone. No, I'm afraid of break-ins, I corrected. I have panic attacks because I'm afraid of break-ins. He leans forward: *But if someone broke in, you wouldn't be alone.*

I don't hear him outside the door, but I know he is there. I splash water over my chest and rub the mud from my heels, between my toes. There are scratches on my knees, shin, feet, but no punctures. I will not die from this.

I put my head below the surface, wet my hair. From underneath the water I see the sun streaming through the bathroom window. He is not standing beneath it now. Another woman might have made another run for it.

But I don't.

86

I come out of the bathroom and there is breakfast. Sections of orange, bread and butter, small packets of jam, are arranged on paper towels at the foot of his bed. I take the curve of orange he offers. Cold in my mouth, it almost hurts. There is no refrigerator, no cooler. Did he leave while I was in the bathroom? Did he want me to think he did? Or is the Someone Who Is Watching retrieving these things?

He offers more orange and I shake my head.

I don't eat much in the morning, I say. Not till I've read the paper.

He nods. Despite the watching, he's still learning. He re-ties my hands and feet. The price I pay for not being hungry. I lie back on the bed and listen to him eat, his jaw a small machine, efficient. I sense he is fuelling up for something.

Do you think they have papers at the motel office?

He looks up and blinks twice, says nothing.

You know, there was no need to call anyone, he says after his last swallow. Your husband will be home in an hour.

No, he won't.

He will.

Well, they could have died in an hour, I say. They could have fallen and cracked their heads open.

He looks at me but says nothing. Probably better he does not. He's not American. Not from the country where you are prosecuted if you leave a child in a stroller while you feed the

87

parking meter. My friend Carrie won't even walk to the mailbox while her infant naps. In his culture, he has been on his own, made his own sandwiches, and watched his brothers and sisters.

How do you know my husband will be home?

It is one of the ransom demands.

The word 'ransom' stands out in his sentence, hangs in the air. He says it oddly, with a lilt, the way some children say candy.

You . . . have kidnapped *me* for ransom? In my sentence, 'me' stands out, incredulous.

He nods, as if it is that simple. As if I just asked if he saw the game last night.

My lower lip quivers. When the tears come, I roll to one side of the bed and let them fall on the scratchy stripes. He hears my small sobs.

He is confused. He offered this as comfort: that it was about money, and not violence, not sex. Not me. Not my little family. But in all the watching, he does not know what I know, and cannot tell him now.

He could not see in Sam, in a few days' or weeks' time, what it's taken me years to comprehend. He doesn't know that our Sub-Zero refrigerator came with a dent along the bottom that saved us 30 per cent. A dent I see first when I walk in the door each night. That our cars are the models the salesmen drive, and came to us with strangers' cigarettes crushed in the ashtray. That Sam goes alone to black tie dinners because he insists that I hate them, when I am convinced, utterly certain, it's because he can wear the same tuxedo but I, photographed, would need a new dress. That our garage holds three sofas from garage sales, their good frames waiting to be reupholstered, changed into Sam's version of new.

He and whomever he is working for – David or anyone else

– have broken a cardinal criminal rule. Never kidnap the family of a man who loves a bargain.

He gets up and brings me a Kleenex from the bathroom.

You should have kept Jamie, I sniffle.

Why?

He might have paid more for her.

Going Home, 2000

Jamie, a wrinkled newborn in a white hat and white receiving blanket, my hands visible at the edge of the frame. Her face is red; she was dressed too warmly for the mild day. I should have known better, but I loved that white set. I always, always had.

It was so unseasonably hot the day I gave birth, Sam and I both wore shorts to the hospital. I was in labour for several hours at home, waiting as long as possible. I knew the maternity ward would not be as comfortable as my own bed.

My moaning finally woke Sam at six. He slept soundly through the groans, the walking back and forth to the bathroom, running the tub. Why didn't I wake him right away? The therapists told me to communicate my needs. 'No one marries a mind reader,' Dr Mueller once said. But no, I wanted Sam to intuit. To know and to sense me struggling next to him.

Isn't that what we all want? To lie next to someone who feels our presence in the bed, who hears our breathing when it goes ragged or deep, who notices our movements as they grow larger and more true, more distinctly ourselves? People change, decades pass. Shouldn't these things register?

As the contractions got closer together, Sam became more nervous, so we went to the hospital. Walking from the car, I stopped twice and bent down for contractions, leaning on brick walls and benches, focused on the cobblestone street. Sam mumbled apologies to the pairs of white legs that passed, as if I'd just vomited in someone's prize roses. A woman in my birthing class said that during her first pregnancy her husband carried her through the hospital lobby and into admitting. It seemed the most absurdly romantic thing I could imagine. It sounded like the next Tiffany ad.

As we waited for the elevator, my waters broke. I felt it trickling down my legs and pooling on the linoleum floor. This was new. This had never happened to me before.

I looked at Sam.

'Don't look, honey,' he said.

It was something he said to me at violent movies, as we passed a car accident, and later, when our daughters would fall. He sensed some things, now and then; he knew what I could and couldn't take. I'd cover my eyes and he would judge it for me, like Josh in the editing room, let me know if it was safe to take it in. He didn't think of it as fear. Fear he didn't understand. Claire is squeamish, he would say to anyone who witnessed it. Once we were at a clambake with live lobsters; I had to walk away. 'My wife flunked biology,' he laughed into the crowd. 'Couldn't dissect a frog!' I considered it an act of kindness, of kinship. The smallest, thinnest of lies.

'Don't look, Claire,' Sam insisted, lifting my chin up with one hand while he punched the elevator button furiously with the other. The water felt like a lake at my feet. 'Don't look, sweetheart.' I shut my eyes as the nurses hurried me into the gown; I tried to avoid seeing my own legs, which I suspected were no longer white.

Dr Malone chose his words carefully, not because I was squeamish, but because he was cautious, knew my history.

One of the few who knew I couldn't bear to lose this baby.

'Your water was tinged with meconium, Claire. We have to hurry now.'

Tinged. A gentle word, far better than stained, rife with, teeming.

The Pitocin he gave me to speed things up made the contractions unbearable. I pitched on the hospital bed, searching for a better position.

When it was time to push, I was exhausted.

'Sam,' I whimpered.

'What, honey, what?'

'I can't do it,' I said.

'Yes, you can. Sure you can. I love you, and I know you can. You're strong, Claire. You are.'

'No, I can't. I can't.'

'Claire,' he said slowly, 'there's no alternative.'

'You do it,' I said, and we all laughed.

I delivered her in two more pushes. Sam cut the cord and they handed her to me. My tears spilled on her downy head, christening her with my hope, my wonder and fear. My arms and chest tingled where I held her, while my lower body ached and shook and leaked. It was hard to concentrate on her while my own body seemed torn in half. I gave her to Sam while the nurse stitched me up.

He carried Jamie around the hospital room and showed her everything in it, pronouncing each word carefully: picture, bed, sink, forceps, mommy, tired tired mommy.

It was something he did every day, until she was old enough to know the names of every complicated thing in our home. Chandelier. Armoire. Soapstone. Flatbed. Backhoe. Skylight.

One morning in January, when she was just ten months old, I put her down on a pile of laundry warm from the dryer. She bounced around in it for a few seconds then crawled away. I heard her crying in the kitchen and found her pulling on the bottom of our old freezer, saying, 'No-ball?'

'Freezer,' I said. 'Freezer.'

I opened it. Sitting next to a tray of ice cubes was a perfectly formed snowball.

'My no-ball,' she said, naming the new thing.

We sat in the frosty air for a long time, watching it in our pyjamas, while a light dusting of snow floated in the wind outside. There was none on the ground. I could imagine Sam grasping at the flakes in the night air, patiently wiping the white dust off tree limbs. I smiled, thinking of how long he had taken, his diligence and care, the sweetness of what he must have said to her afterwards.

'Snow-ball. Jamie's snow-ball. Let's put it in the freezer so it will last until I get back home again.

'Home from my trip.'

The room smells of orange. He's outside on his cell phone for most of the morning and I have a lot of time to think. Dangerous for me, thinking. I imagine the original scenario, my daughter taken, me fighting. Him knocking me down when I try to stop him, hitting me hard with an open hand, outrunning me, Jamie screaming. This seems ridiculous to me now, a bad movie you watch on cable.

I picture the flyers: would Sam dare to distribute one, with 'Missing' above a photo of me? Even with the haircut and the years of worry lines settled into my forehead, I still look a bit like the girl David knew. And what about the other flyer, the one that says 'Wanted', Jamie's description of him: hazel eyes, light brown skin, black hair. His kindness, his manners, wouldn't show in the police sketch. They are trained to see the worst in people, like me.

And where would they look for us first? The garage, the neighbourhood, the office? I imagine Michael and Josh pointing out my desk, hands going through my pens, vitamins, tampons. The detectives would have my briefcase from the den, my story notes about child labour. Michael would tell them it was just an idea. Children missing fingers. No story there yet. Josh would pipe in on my behalf, say that I hadn't had time to do all the research yet. That I was looking into cultural differences about how early Amish boys are considered men in their families. They'd hold up the photo of the Tiffany man and ask if I was doing a story on jewellery. No, Josh would say. Would he mention the man who'd been snooping around, asking questions? Yes, I think he would; Josh was thorough.

Next stop: the gym. My yoga teacher would recognize my picture. Oh, yes, Claire. She's very flexible but she leaves before we do headstands because she's afraid of having a stroke.

And what about Ally and Carrie: *I haven't seen her in weeks. We're so busy! The baby was sick and the washer is flooding and work has been insane!* And the guilt, yes, there would at least be that. Back when Sam travelled infrequently, they would sleep over: a slumber party with salmon and wine. When the policemen interview them they'll be shocked that what I'd told them after the third bottle of wine had come true: someone *was* out to get me after all.

On some level they didn't understand, tucked into their beds with their husbands at their side and their alarm systems beaming across each window. Carrie's driveway had an electronic gate, a fence with iron points and an intercom. Ally's husband was a former Green Beret. I remember watching a reality show with them, the kind where you choose a fiancé from a selected group.

She's going to choose Ryan, Ally insisted. He makes her feel safe.

No, no, Carrie said. Her family loves Charlie. And Charlie makes her laugh.

If she wants to laugh, she can go to a comedy club, I say.

Carrie countered with: If she wants to feel safe, she should just hire a bodyguard.

I looked at the screen, watching for some symbol of what made a man exude that quality. If you could see safety in a man, what would it look like? Was it size or simmering righteous anger?

I am tired now, hungry. The room feels smaller, the bedspread scratchier. I try to read his lips, can't. Is he negotiating my release, or my stay? I imagine a ridiculous conversation: he is talking to his mother or girlfriend. How's work today, baby? Fine, same old same old. Might run late tonight. Don't hold dinner.

I'm just a little filing that he's behind on. I am his overtime.

He comes back in, digs under the bed. Aha, I think. He has run out of space, finally, in those pockets. Is there a cooler under there? My stomach growls loudly.

He looks up at me holding my stomach, laughs. He's one of those men with a little boy laugh – higher pitched than his voice, almost a giggle. Another detail.

I'll get lunch soon, he says. He unchains my feet, tells me I can stretch for a minute.

He pulls a notebook and pen from underneath the bed, and goes back outside to use his phone. Watching, I'm jealous of the ballpoint pressed against the paper. I would like to write a letter, make a grocery list, start the child labour story. I miss not only the newspaper, but pen and paper and magazines and lip balm and baby wipes and pink Barbie panties in my big black bag.

Outside, his back is to the window. My moment, I suddenly think. Not for escape, but knowledge, information. I would settle for distraction. There is something *under there*.

I scoot to the end of my warm bed and swing over to his cold one. In one roll, one slide, I am on the floor. I lift the bedspread with my feet and peer underneath. No cooler; there is not enough overhead clearance. Instead, there is a flat canvas rectangle. Green or brown, I can't tell. It reminds me of the insulated carriers you take to pot-luck dinners.

I hear his footsteps outside. The walls, the windows, that thin.

Instinctively, I hit the floor and start to roll. I'm all the way around his bed and in the space between them when he walks in.

His eyes scan the room. He takes two steps, looks down.

I look up. I see him differently from below. The curve of his jaw, his nostrils, his cheekbones. The ceiling is glittery, cheap but festive above his head. He is not angry, but confused. And perhaps, I think, mildly amused.

I fell off the bed, I say.

He reaches out a hand to help me up. Duty, what he does. The same surety to his movement that I sensed as he tied the knots, checked for tightness.

As he lowers me back on the bed it reminds me of something, someone. The efficiency, the strength. I'm pregnant with Jordan, my contractions begin in a cab. The ambulance drivers who meet me on the corner. The lowering into a stretcher, hoisting, arranging.

Are you a paramedic? I blurt out.

What? His head whips around.

A paramedic or a—

Don't be silly, he says too quickly.

And I know. Finally, I know *something*. Maybe not a paramedic, but a nurse, an orderly, something close. I can tell by his voice.

But I can't put two and two together. How would a person with those skills connect to a person with Sam's? If David hired him, why someone like him to threaten me and not a thug? The triangle suddenly slams together in my head: I imagine ampoules in the container beneath the bed. Phials, syringes. The lethal intersection of paramedic and kidnapper and pharmaceutical executive. His box.

I turn away. I feel it coming the way some people feel an earthquake gathering force. My shivering knocks the headboard against the wall. On the ground, his feet shudder as if a large truck rumbles past.

Are you all right? he asks quietly.

You, I say between chattering teeth, are going to drug me

and take me to the next location. You are going to kill me slowly instead of all at once.

He steps toward me, curls a corner of my bedspread over my legs.

You, he replies, have quite an imagination.

For lunch he orders what I ask him for, exactly: turkey with avocado and tomato, crisp fries. In the bag I find salt, napkins and water. The avocado is soft and nutty, like a delicacy from another world. I appreciate it as if it's my first taste. He lets me watch TV, like a child home from school. An old movie with Michelle Pfeiffer and Sean Penn. I've seen it before; I've already cried over its sentimental ending but I don't care. I pretend I don't know what's coming.

He keeps the remote to prevent me from changing the channel and seeing the news. No matter: I can imagine the newscast in my head. I look at him and try to turn him into a drawing. Will Jamie have seen him as I see him? Reduced to pencil, what's left is what's strong: cheekbones, chin, hands. Or as a little girl might: the world of men divided into monster and daddy, and this one man who stands in between. Who is he to her, to us?

Wanted. So it will say on the news.

I don't watch news at night any more; only in the morning. I had a theory that violent images somehow got trapped in my head. I let them rattle around by day, but they altered my thinking at night. I started by cutting out news, then ten o'clock drama shows about police, hospital, and forensics. I tried to remove all scary movies but this wasn't completely possible. There was always an injury, a car crash, something that freaked me out. I'd reach frantically for the remote, switch to something funny, fast. The girls would find me at 7 a.m., wrapped in a blanket with the remote in my hand, the television still tuned to Nick at Nite.

Now I only watch romantic comedies. No war movies, no mysteries, no international submarine thrillers. He has chosen appropriately for me. The most violent thing that happens is Sean Penn falling on the floor while Aimee Mann sings a Beatles song.

You like these kinds of movies. He says it from the other bed as a statement, not a question.

I turn to him. Is this the face that watched me through the window while I watched movies? He rubs his hands across his chin: was that the sound I heard in the bushes when I got up to check? From the shrubbery, through the hedges, between the leaves, through the two panes of glass, yes, I'm certain, all these movies look alike to him.

What kind of movies? I say dismissively.

The kind, he says evenly, with the happy endings.

After the movie, *Jeopardy* comes on and the theme music lulls me to sleep. The questions and answers, the rhythm of the show, finds its way in to my brain. I dream I am taking a test. I know the answers but I can't lift the pen. A high school dream, but the same as so many others: I can't scream, I can't move, I can't write. A dream of impotence. I expect one night to dream I'm an ice sculpture.

I wake up damp. My hair sticks to the thin pillowcase, my legs to the scratchy striped bedspread. I haven't napped since Jordan was a baby, and we curled into one another in milky exhaustion.

I lift my head and look out the window. It's twilight and I'm alone. The TV is turned off; the remote is not nearby. At work I've walked by the lunchroom, peered in as people watched their mid-day soap operas. It was something to get used to, working at a local station, being tethered to a place. People didn't gather in bars or hotel lobbies to catch up and scatter; they stuck to one another in corridors and lunchrooms, found small luxuries wherever they could: a drawer full of chocolates, television at lunchtime. A luxury, to watch TV in the afternoon, I always thought.

There is no laundry to fold, no bills to be paid. I point my toes, stretch my arms overhead. I may be trussed, but I'm free to spend my afternoons doing nothing.

I think of my yoga teacher, whispering as we all held a shaky pose. We put ourselves in little boxes, she says. How will you do in your box? I breathe deeply as I stretch again. It is not an entirely uncomfortable box I'm in.

I stand up and hop over to the window. The Cutlass is still there, but I don't see him. My heart speeds up. I don't open the door, the window. I don't run or scream. Amazing, but this is what I do: I drop to the ground near his bed and lift the bed-spread. I pull out the quilted bag with my feet. Green, I see now. It is hard to open it while encumbered, but I force myself. I want to see inside this magician's bag, the black silk sack adapted for modern criminal life.

I'd like to tell you I opened it looking for a tool or weapon. I'd like to think that was buried in the back of my mind. But in the front, there was only desperate, crippling curiosity. What was he hiding from me? Who sent him? Why did he take me?

Beyond the drugs and syringes, what I feared, I don't know what I expected. A disassembled rifle? Newspaper clippings? A little black book?

I don't see those things. It's possible they are underneath; the bag is layered and stacked. On top are legal pads, yellow and lined. And next to them are videotapes, labelled in orange marker: 1, 2, 3. I see all the way to 8.

Outside the Cutlass door closes. Like a child I grab some-thing: Tape #1. I zip up the bag, kick it back, then scoot along the carpet, pushing the tape with my fingers as I go. When I hear footsteps on the sidewalk, I swat the tape, my hands like table football flippers, aiming underneath my own bed. I don't know how far it travels, but I can't see it beneath the bedspread. Good.

The footsteps stop; the Cutlass door opens, then shuts. I rise to my feet, a small struggle. For a moment I stand, taking the time I don't have, allowing myself to think. It could be him, or it could be someone else. Someone watching.

My eyes go to the only thing that stands between us. A door. Have I looked at it before now?

It's darker in places than others. It looks heavy, but almost certainly is not. There is no plastic 'Do Not Disturb' sign hanging on the cheap gold knob. Of course not; it is hanging outside the door. Was that the very first thing he did? It's possible he paid the maid off; I haven't even heard a cart rumble past. Near the top of the door are four holes where the chain lock used to be. Of course: he must leave now and then, and I must not lock him out.

I go back to my bed, holding my breath, wondering who I hear.

A few seconds later, he slides in again.

Each time, it is getting easier.

TUESDAY

I don't know if he sleeps.

He lies down each night on the bed next to mine, but when I wake up he is always gone.

I'm too tired to do the obvious thing: wait until I hear his breathing settle, try to escape. Each time I consider doing this, I fall asleep. I blame it on the rope, the nightgown. Constricted and dressed for bed. My body was just doing what it was told: Don't move. Sleep. He may as well have taped my eyes shut.

When I wake in the middle of the night, shaking from a nightmare, scared of the dark, he is always sitting outside, near the car. It makes me believe there are a lot of vacancies here in Mid-County.

He leaves me alone a lot, which could be interpreted as trust. Or nonchalance. Fear of intimacy. One of my therapists might say he was giving me opportunity to escape. The bathroom window, beckoning. I can't forget the third thing in his list, the truest thing: *We're being watched*. They could be guarding me in shifts. You take the back I'll take the front. He could be sleeping in the car while The Other One watches the door.

After two nights together, we have rituals now. The lights left on, the chaining and unchaining of wrists to headboard. The turns taken in the bathroom. We could continue on this way, in a rhythm, no surprises. Two people, I know, can go on like this indefinitely.

When I wake up Tuesday morning, it's already light, and

he's outside on the phone. The Cutlass is wet from dew or rain. In the bathroom it has also rained: the thin white mat is down; his wet footprints intrude on the pile. I've never slept through one of Sam's early morning showers. I wake when he wakes. Restless. A light sleeper. I see now that I've labelled myself incorrectly. I stretch. Lift my legs and hands simultaneously, as one. It pulls my lower stomach muscles: kidnapping crunches.

He comes in with something wrapped in tissue under his arm. He starts to hand it to me, then remembers the limitations of my hands, and puts it on my lap.

His eyes smile as I unroll it.

My white T-shirt, my grey knit capris.

The blonde hairs on my arms stand upright. When did he take my clothes? Before? After? He has been in my house *twice*?

My lower lip quivers. I think of the nights just before the storm, before he came. The nightmares, pounding heart, twisted sheets. The sounds I thought I heard, talked myself out of. It's more than I can bear, believing I was right.

His brow is knitted. He says a half-sentence: I thought you would. Trails off.

These are mine?

Yes.

You went through my closet? You say this isn't about me, yet you go through my closet, my things?

He blinks, shakes his head. I went to the Gap.

He reaches in his right cargo pocket and pulls out the price tags. The plastic tabs still dangling like fish on a line.

They looked like what you wear, he says quietly.

Our eyes meet. I see the pattern the last few days: he has tried to throw right thing after wrong.

He goes in to fill the tub. Halfway through, he bends down, swirls his forearm in the water to check its heat. A familiar pose, so classic it could be modelled in clay.

Do you have children? I blurt out.

110

He stands up, hand dripping. There is something in his eyes that looks like pain but could be anger. He says nothing. I've gone too far, I know.

With my wrists free, I carry the new clothes into the bathroom, set them down. From the bathtub they are a beautiful sight. I think of my antique drawers full of flat modern shapes. He knows the truth: I don't waltz around in pink silk nightgowns.

He closes the bathroom door. Trusting?

I dry myself off, unfold the T-shirt. It's one size smaller than the one in my drawer, whiter, less soft. Inside the last fold is a pair of white panties and a toothbrush. It tumbles to the ground, lays there like evidence.

I walk out, my hair still dripping. A wet V forms on my back.

I hold the toothbrush aloft. We're staying? I ask.

He looks up from his notepad. In one way or another, it is a question I'll ask every day until we are both tired of the answer.

He breathes in before he looks up. Something he does before he speaks.

I got his voicemail.

Is he home yet?

He shrugs.

He can't get his messages in the air, I say, sitting down on my bed.

He looks at me, says nothing.

They make you turn off your phone, I add.

The look he shoots me is almost amusement.

I stop defending my husband to my kidnapper. It's not in my best interest to take sides.

Dr Kearny said fighting was my defence mechanism. I think of this trait as part of me: like an upturned nose or sprinkle of freckles. I live in a neighbourhood surrounded by kindness. Charity events. Fund-raisers. Volunteers. I am not that nice.

Mommy, why aren't you like other mommies? Jamie asked

111

when she went to school. Other mommies are boring, I replied. And what I didn't say: Other mothers take their husband's name because they were proud of it, and not because they had something to hide.

He locks me in for a minute, then comes back with breakfast. I imagine it was in the car, or the Man He's In Cahoots With brought it. I thought he might have taken my hint about the newspaper yesterday, but no. There is nothing but food in the white bag, the plastic containers of yogurt and cantaloupe clicking against the spoon. At the bottom is another orange.

The silver phone rings and he goes to the door. I pick up the orange. Dense, juicy, a cold weight in my hand. The back of his head calls to me briefly. How hard, how fast could I throw it? He turns suddenly and I put it down. My thumb travels along the handle of the spoon, up the roughly cut tip. It is irregular there, cuts me with little effort. The spoon should be easy to hide. His second line beeps. After he says hello, he goes in the bathroom and closes the door, turns on the fan.

My heart races; is it Sam calling back? Nervous, like that flutter when he called me the first time after Ally's party. I remember picking up the phone, hearing his smooth voice. *Claire? Dr Spin here.* And after that first surge of joy, I felt that fear again, the questions he could ask. The men from my past appeared in my head, dishevelled, in a row, like a police line-up. Eventually he would ask about the scar. Who wouldn't?

I slide the spoon under my pillow, lean closer to the door. All I can hear is tin fan flying. I imagine if I dared to hop over to the door and press my ear against it, he would turn on the faucet, too. He is in the bathroom a long time. Five minutes? It is long for a man to talk on the phone. For this reason alone, I doubt he is talking to Sam. I lean against the headboard and deflate.

When he comes back there is colour in his cheeks. He looks out the window and sips coffee.

What's wrong? I say. It's not the first time I've been in a motel room with a man fairly bursting with a secret.

Was that Sam?

He turns to me with his reddened cheeks.

It was his secretary.

Now I know: the flush is anger, not heat, not embarrassment. Sam has put him on the level of gardener, carpenter, maid. Reduced.

I ask what she said, but I really wanted to know how she said it. Did beautiful Melanie lose her calm, her commanding tone? Did the ice of her voice melt even a little?

She said Sam would call me in five minutes. After his *press conference. Before he goes to New York.*

He sits down on the other bed.

Maybe she thought it was a joke.

Yeah, maybe.

I hand him back the orange peel, the empty containers.

His face surveys the interior of the bag. Where is the spoon?

I shrug.

His left hand scrabbles beneath my pillow. He pulls the spoon out and dangles it in front of me, his head tsk-tsking in a similar rhythm.

He stands so close I can't see his right foot; it's partially under the bed. Suddenly he looks down and I have a half-second of panic about the videotape. Then he scratches his ankle with the spoon.

What exactly were you going to do with this? he asks. Eat me?

Dig my way out, I reply.

And go where, exactly?

Somewhere I could get a newspaper. I smile.

Santa Fe, 1999

Sam and his business partner, Hugh, at an arts festival. They are almost as tan as the Native American artist they are speaking to. Hugh was scheduled to be keynote speaker at The National Public Relations Conference, where there was very little actual conferring. Lots of sightseeing, golfing and spa treatments, Sam had said, after convincing me to tag along. Hugh hadn't married Anne yet, and I felt like a third wheel. The people in his field bored me; they talked endlessly about wine cellars and stocks.

I met Hugh the same night I met Sam, at Ally's party. When I left to go to the bathroom, Sam was alone; when I came back he was a matched set.

'You two look like brothers,' I said as I shook Hugh's hand and tried not to stare.

'I'm younger,' Sam said quickly, and we all laughed. But when you looked more closely, you could tell it was true. Younger, thinner, more boyish. Sam had a spring in his step; Hugh moved more slowly.

'Watch out for that one,' Hugh sighed as Sam went to get us another round of g and ts. 'A woman is no match for charming self-promotion.'

I should have listened more carefully: it was a warning: AOL keyword: self. I didn't see it that way at the time. Sam's energy was infectious. He believed politicians could win, that new products could launch, that fledgling theatre companies could thrive. Sam was the spinning top at the centre of them all. He couldn't walk a single city block in any north-eastern city without running into someone he knew.

My job at the television station was the opposite of his: it required no travel, and a focus on facts, not perceptions. I spent most of my time writing, editing, making phone calls. He would die doing my job. He needed people, and he needed fantasies, like the rest of us need air.

Sam never fit in at my office; the women I worked with were married to musicians and painters. I pictured them in their beds at night, reading sonnets, looking out the window at the moon. They were alike, but too alike could be dull, I knew. Sam and I were yin and yang; a better team, I thought, at first. A blending of different strengths.

He tried, though, to appear similar to me. Not lying, exactly, but angling things, slanting them. He was the first man I ever met who pretended to be intellectual. He was good at it, too: it took me years to find him out. His older brother Robert, also friends with Hugh, graduated at the top of his class at Princeton; Sam went to San Diego State. Sam did whatever he could to keep up the appearance of being as smart as his brother, or as smart as me. He subscribed to *Harper's*, spread the issues on the coffee table. He bought cheap prints of famous paintings and hung them in his condo. He carried the *Wall Street Journal* on the train, but at the end of the day it looked smooth, unread.

Hugh had the money, Sam had the energy. Did they need anything else, really? Together they built a hugely successful business on top of their friendship and their hobbies. It's that simple. It's almost as if they asked themselves: What can we do that involves golfing, fishing, eating and drinking all week long?

That's what I think on the bad days. I see the posing in every frame.

Sam wooed me with the Cliff Notes version of literature, films, art. He aired other people's opinions. Felt what critics told him to feel. Living with him has been like living with a lab experiment. Double-blind testing. Findings reconfirmed over time. Actual results may vary with a different wife. But I'm the one he has: the only one he has ever had. I'm still learning why he chose me, or if he did. It is entirely possible that Hugh told him he should marry that girl, so he did.

The first night, when Hugh warned me about Sam, it was clear Sam had been similarly informed.

'So you're the infamous Claire.' He smiled when he took my hand.

'I'm not that infamous,' I said quietly.

'All that travelling, the awards? You're like a character in a Tom Clancy novel.'

Ugh, I made a face, and he immediately adjusted his point of reference.

'Okay, Dickens? Chekhov?'

I smiled, assuming he was well-read, which mattered to me. Mattered more than it should have. Maybe that's the way I should view it, not that Sam was a poseur, but that I was a snob.

'I prefer Tennessee Williams.' I smile. 'Or Mamet. Mamet is good.'

'Indeed,' he replied.

The one word guaranteed to flag intelligence, knowing, and sympathy at the same time. Sam used it as cover. I'm going in. In over my head.

Why was I surprised? Nothing is as you picture it. That is the only truth I'd want my daughters to find in the closet. The true meaning inside the box. The warm cookies, the picket fence, the wagging tail on the porch. They are never as beautiful as when they are viewed from the road.

117

The rain stops gradually, moving from downpour to drizzle to nothing. I watch this as I watch everything, through a two-inch opening in the curtain. It provides a vertical stripe of light that changes from greenish grey to blue to orange. If something happened – if the Someone Who Is Watching walked by, or a travelling salesman's car glided through the parking lot, or a damn housekeeper cared if the kidnapper needed towels – it would feel like the thinnest of stages. A secret could be revealed in the second act. A new character could walk on or off. The lighting changes but not the props. The Cutlass looks misty every morning, but it's from dew. Its blue metallic paint is not a good measurement tool: no way to tell the temperature or the time. The motel window faces east, I know that from the sun. I can tell by the way his shirt billows when he walks outside that the wind is coming from the north. All those high school science classes. They come into play the moment you are kidnapped.

Does it sound boring? It wasn't at first. I'm accustomed to seeing only slices of the world. I fear it in its entirety; there is plenty I'm not ready to take in. Still, the days were not short. I could have used a few more distractions.

After breakfast his phone rings three separate times and each time he walks to the door, takes the call outside. He turns to me before he opens the door, looking at me as if to say: it's not him. And by the way, I know you are watching through the window.

The ring on his Motorola phone is a liquidy bloop, subtler than other rings he might have chosen. The musical ones drive me insane; I'm grateful he doesn't have one. I assume the calls, while not Sam, are still about me. I could be wrong. He could have overdue library books, dentist appointments, an irate girlfriend telling him he loves his work more than her.

I've been separated from my own phones – work, home, cell. Maybe thirty messages at work alone. The police are puzzling over them now, deciding which to keep and which to throw away. That I don't miss: the listening, passwording, archiving. And I don't miss the ringing. When he was home, Sam always answered the phone, and I always let the machine screen it. He was stunned by that, how I could let things go. Phone, mail. He was like a child with them both: he still believed something wonderful could arrive in an envelope. I remember his face, almost giddy as he tore open the envelopes. Whistling through what could have been a chore. You may already have won. Enclosed please find. Before the girls could read or spell, he'd always hand them something from the pile to keep: Look, Jamie, Saks sent you a shoe catalogue! And, Julia, I believe this magazine is addressed to you!

Some days I left the mail up in the box, just forgot it. At Christmas I groaned over the flow of boxes from UPS. Now, I miss the mail; would give anything for a magazine or catalogue. Paper. I need paper.

It's quiet in the motel room. The phone, ripped from the wall, is silent. It will bring neither good news nor bad. I picture the do not disturb sign swinging on the knob. No news will come in that way either. We will not be disturbed from our crime.

The orange lamp sits on a nightstand with one drawer. The drawer slides open easily, and I find the expected black Bible. I lay it on the bed. It is annoying to turn the pages of a new book when you are tied up. The spine is stiff; the pages keep flopping closed. I stop trying.

My eyes fix on the television set, as if my wishing could turn it on. The remote, I know, is in his pocket. Underneath the TV, between it and the chest of drawers it sits on, is a black box I thought was for the cable. I see now that it is larger: a DVD? No, a VCR.

My breath deepens as I sit up. Did I know, subconsciously, that it was there when I grabbed that tape? Audio-video equipment could not be standard issue at the Mid-County. There was no mini-bar, no shoeshine bag, no thick white robe mono-grammed 'MC'. He'd brought it in, rigged it with something out of his cargo pocket. The Lindbergh kidnapper crossed with a handyman. My toes wriggle between the draped hem of the bedspread and the carpet. My right pinkie toe hits the edge of my hidden videotape.

Outside, he shouts. I pull my feet up. Caught already. I peer out the curtain. His hand chops the air as he yells in gestures that match his angry Spanish. I assume it's Spanish and not Italian; I only know French from my work over there. I dig back to remember: does David speak any languages other than French? After a minute he snaps the phone shut, groans in frustration to the sky. He turns and looks through the curtain. Our eyes line up in that space. We see each other across a very uncrowded room. Then, there is something he retrieves in the car. I assume he is coming right back. I don't move. I wait. I'm rooted to the spot by my curiosity as much as my rope handcuffs.

It's a while before he comes back. Five minutes? Ten? The small increments of time have slipped away from me now. It is simply morning, afternoon, night. Breakfast, lunch, dinner.

He opens the door and looks at me strangely.

You haven't moved, he says.

121

My toes have touched your damn hidden tape, I want to say, but simply shrug. How is it possible to disappoint or surprise someone who doesn't know you?

He sits on his bed, runs one hand across his mouth. The way all men do.

Was that Sam you were yelling at?

He shakes his head.

You've had a lot of calls.

He turns to me, considers. To tell her or not to tell her. I'm a popular guy, he says.

You're an angry guy.

He swallows. My boss is not happy with me, he says.

I blink. It's the first time he's used that term. His boss. The one who is watching?

Tell me who you work for, I say quietly.

Sure. He swallows. If you tell me who David is.

Our eyes meet. My head shakes no. Debate over. I should not be surprised, this expectation of tit for tat. It's the currency of kidnapping.

Is your boss angry because of me?

He nods.

I am his mistake, the reason he will be fired.

The weight of it sits in the room, the importance of a good outcome. Bigger than a product launch or off-site meeting. If he messes this up, we are all in deep shit.

My foot suddenly itches so badly I can hardly stand it. I squirm, try to rub it against the bed frame. He looks at me wriggling, swings his legs over his bed gracefully, so gracefully I envy his ability to move. He picks up my bound feet and scratches the top of them both, briskly, efficiently. His nails are short and even, the fingertips smooth.

The phone rings again. He puts my feet down, opens it, answers with a sigh in Spanish.

Thank you, I call out, as he moves toward the door.

Before he opens it, he looks back at me and nods once. I know the nod does not mean you're welcome.

It means Sam.

Afternoon.

Lunch.

Get me a paper! I call out.

Jamie at the ballgame with Daddy, 2007

She smiles in the photo, waving a pennant. But she ate two
spires of candy floss and on the drive home Sam saw her face
turn pale in the rear-view mirror, and pulled to the shoulder in
the nick of time. I remember laughing afterwards at Sam's
description of the blue vomit.

Sam was good with illness, emergencies. I was not, and the
girls knew it. When you are a parent, there is no statute of
limitations on mistakes. You kiss your three-year-old's head
and apologize, say that Mommy is sorry, that Mommy is
stressed, and she says that's okay. You know better: you know
when she is twenty, or forty, one of these moments will come
back to her on a therapist's couch.

Julia is four and has had a stomach ache all day.

'My tummy hurts,' she says again at nine thirty. I perform
the same series of moves I had several times that day: kiss
head, no fever. Touch her belly button and ask if that's where
it hurts. 'Yes.' Ask if she is sure she doesn't have to go to the
bathroom. 'No. I don't, Mommy.'

No bleeding, no fever, no pain on the right side. 'Go back
to bed, honey,' I tell her, 'and try sleeping with your knees up
to your chest. Maybe it's just some gas in your tummy.'

An hour later she emerges in tears, bent over at the
waist.

'I tried, Mommy, I did. But all I can think of is knives in my tummy,' she sobs.

In her eyes I recognize, suddenly, the look of escalating fear. No child, I thought, would have those thoughts unless something was wrong. Terribly, deeply wrong.

I put my work aside, turn off the dryer, let the washer continue to spin. I pack a diaper, a bottle, my phone. Jamie and Jordan are sweaty with sleep, and look at me as if I'm a stranger when I pull them from their beds.

By the time we reach the ER parking lot, the baby has resettled into sleep. I take the stroller from the back and lift her into it, praying she does not awaken. I tell Jamie to push the stroller while I carry Julia.

In the waiting room, a man sits with a bandaged hand; I don't look at it. In the corner, by the television, a teenage girl sleeps in a circle, like a dog.

We sign in and wait. The TV is muted; a talk show with no talk. There are no magazines except *Fortune* and *Golf*. Jamie rubs her eyes, I rub Julia's back. A yawning nurse calls the bandaged hand man, then us.

'I think it's her appendix,' I say to the resident.

We are stuffed into the examining room: the stroller barely fits in the corner. I pull up the sunshade against the bright hospital light.

The doctor's eyes don't even widen. 'Do you now?' His accent is British or South African, I can't tell which.

He takes her temperature, thumps her chest, her throat. Asks her the same questions I did: where, how long. And a few new ones: 'What did you eat and drink? Did you go to school today? A playdate?'

He snaps off his glove and looks at me too kindly.

'I'm going to give her a suppository and let's wait half an hour.'

'A suppository for fever?' I ask.

126

'No fever,' he says evenly. 'Her bowel is distended. Probably nothing, but there's a slim possibility of an—'

'Obstruction?'

'Yes. But as I said, unlikely. Why don't you rest for a half-hour or so? If she has to evacuate, don't flush. I'll need to have a look.'

He turned off the lights and drew the curtain.

Twenty minutes later Julia sits up, says she has to go to the bathroom. I go with her and it's suddenly obvious: she'd been constipated for days.

We leave after being reminded to eat more fibre and less cheese. I exchange a look with the nurse, who has clearly had a four-year-old in the house. Pizza and macaroni cheese and string cheese. What else do children eat?

We pull in the driveway. This is how children get stolen, I think as I prop the door open at 1 a.m. and leave two children sleeping in the car while I carry one in.

Sam plops into bed beside me at 6 a.m., an hour before I need to get up. He complains of snoring passengers on the red-eye.

I tell him about my evening, thinking I have him beat.

His brow is knitted at the beginning; he asks caring questions. 'Did she vomit? How was she the day before? Poor baby.'

But at some point, his forehead wrinkles, as if he knows there is not a good ending.

'Wow, I hope the insurance company pays for it,' he says. 'They're picky about non-emergencies now.'

'I'm sure they'll pay. She'd been sick all day.'

'That could be a thousand-dollar enema, Claire. A thousand dollars.'

I want to ask him what he would have done in my place, but it is an impossible question. He is not in my place. He is never in my place.

I lie back down and wait for some alarm to go off. Mine, his, the baby monitor, the smoke alarm, the carbon monoxide detector. Something that signals I should get up and leave the room.

But it doesn't come, and I stay. For the moment, I stay.

The air conditioner rumbles against the wall. The wall complains against the air conditioner. They are locked in their loud battle. I want to cover my ears and can't. When I lift my palms to my chin, my fingers barely graze my ears. The smallest things elude me, thanks to the ropes around my wrists. He unchains me for small periods of time, but there are still the damned home-made handcuffs.

The rain has passed and the heatwave is back; I felt the rush when he opened the door. But the air conditioner has fought valiantly, and it is freezing inside now, the way only a motel room can be freezing. I spin like an alligator, trying to create warmth inside the threadbare sheets. The layers on top of me – sheet, blanket, spread – are just different variations of thin. Somehow I maneuvre the pillow against my ear. Warmer. Quieter. No more angry Spanish from outside. I know so little of that language – the only words I can remember are the ones Jamie and Julia learned in school. *Blanco. Motocycletta*. I don't hear them.

Spinning back to the window, I don't see him between the curtains, but I know he is near. I would have heard the Cutlass, even through the pillows. He is gone longer this time.

Instead of fishing the tape out from beneath my bed, hopping over to the VCR and watching it, I do the cowardly thing. I imagine it. I'm certain it is surveillance footage of my own home, family and yard. There is no other explanation.

Still, there were a lot of tapes in the bag. Could this be larger than me? Were there other homes targeted? Calculations are in my head: his precision, his foreign-ness. His anger with Sam. With a chill, I remember what he said the first night: *Americans spoil their children*. Sam has travelled to Mexico, to Venezuela, to Cuba, even, for business. Three times? Four? I can't remember. He is often on a red-eye; do the red-eyes come from Mexico? He and Hugh have two other business partners in his firm, all married, each with children. Were they involved too?

Our entourage will grow. We will need a suite. We will need a wing. We will have to bribe the manager and vending machine operators as well as the housekeepers of the Mid-County Motor Inn. I remember the sign as we pulled in the first night: 'Vacancy.' Does it say 'No' now?

He kicks the door open, throws his phone on his bed. It ricochets against the wooden headboard, lands spinning on the nightstand. My pillow goes to my eyes, trying to protect myself. After a few seconds, I allow myself a peek.

He stands in front of the window, staring out at his own bad luck. I know this part. I have been here before: two men, fighting over me, and I am with the angry one. Violence, jealousy, rage. There is nothing that can't happen when you let two boyfriends overlap. It is as dangerous as owning two tigers. Isn't it, David?

I shiver beneath the covers, squeeze the pillow to quiet my chattering teeth. If I spoke they would punctuate my sentences in odd places, pebbles around my tongue. But I know better than to open my mouth.

I hear fabric rustling, sliding. He walks to me, pulls the pillow away from my face. I wince.

He drops a navy blue sweatshirt on my chest and walks back to the window.

Thank you, I say. It's unzipped already, so I position the fleecy inside around my neck. After a few minutes my shivering subsides.

He looks out at the parking lot with one hand on his hip, girlish, unusual for him.

What's wrong? I say.

Your husband, he begins. Does he . . . appreciate you?

The tears come to say what I can't. How long would he have had to watch us to suspect what I suspect? I watched for years before I saw a thing. The excuses: he's just practical; he's not particularly sentimental; he's just busy, preoccupied.

Did he ask if I was hurt? I blurt out.

He hesitates. Yes, of course.

I assume, I sniff, that you are asking him for money?

Partly.

What else?

A change in business practices.

My eyes narrow; my forehead wrinkles. On Sunday I thought I was taken to be killed, by Monday I knew it was money, assumed it was revenge. But now, on Tuesday: a crusade?

A change in the way Sam gets publicity? I sit up now, the sweatshirt dangling off my shoulders.

You don't know, do you?

Don't know what?

What your husband does for a living.

He has a public relations company. I realize how stupid I sound.

Our eyes meet. My mouth, still open, moves again.

Are you a client of Sam's?

He laughs that boyish laugh.

Your boss, I mean.

He speaks to the window. This is not very American, this not knowing. It is very old world, the man conducting his nasty business, the woman not asking about the blood on his hands. Look at you. You are no modern American woman.

No, I think. The only blood I can picture on Sam's hands is from the jaw of a fish.

131

I shake my head. No. You must be mista—

I am *not*.

I thought of Sam's office, the two floors with the sweeping views, the sleek lobby, the modern furniture. Art on the walls, flowers on the desks. Hugh chose beautiful things. There was a silver plaque on their door with both of their names on it. And on each desk, thick embossed business cards. Chairs that were good for bad backs. There were people there. Men shaking hands. Well-dressed girls with their young shiny skin, talking on headsets, arranging things. Were they all actors?

What business is he in, then?

He shakes his head. I'm in enough hot water already.

His boss will be angrier now. He imagined a simpler trans-action: a child with no muscles or scheming mind, a father with a broken heart. Instead, they have me, a panicky woman of questionable worth, trying to think my way out. Following the concentric circles between WASPy public relations pundit and crusading Latino paramedic. Where is the overlap?

What did you tell your boss?

It is his turn to be confused. About what?

About taking me instead of Jamie. What reason did you give?

The reasons don't matter.

They do if you care what he thinks of you.

He says nothing, so I continue. If you tell him the truth, I say, that I begged you, he will think one thing. And if you tell him that Jamie was vomiting and having a seizure, he will think another. If you tell him I have family money, he will think something else altogether.

Do you have a recommendation? he asks, mildly amused. There is a tilt to his lip that gives him away. He likes this kind of play.

I would say a combination of two and three.

He nods, turns. Comes back to sit on his bed.

I told him she wasn't in her bed, he says. That I found her in your bed, and you woke up.

That sounds plausible, I say.

We are two people in separate beds, discussing nightly crimes.

Yes.

Why would he be mad about that?

He said I should have beaten you unconscious and taken her.

My breath catches in my chest. I finger my necklace again, feel the frisson against my throat. Threats. Tough talk: God, that sounds like David. *I'm going to beat you within an inch of your life. If you leave you will be sorry the rest of your days.* But David's complaints, David's anger, don't line up anywhere near Sam's business. Or do they?

I look at him. He looks back at me. A curl of his lip, a set of his jaw. He wants me to believe he could beat me and put me in the trunk, but chose not to, so I would owe him. He wants me to feel the swelling, the dark colours rising beneath my skin. A man with his background would know what to do and exactly when to stop. If there are evil nurses and doctors, so there might be evil paramedics.

I shudder and look away. What he wants. I feel him watching me, satisfied I'm still afraid of him.

To my right I'm aware of his hand shuffling in his cargo pocket. Change, metal, paper, mixed together without belonging, stirred up, protesting. It is the sound of immigration, integration, frustration. Then it stops.

There is a shadow on my cheek. I turn. He holds out a bundle that looks like mail.

An olive branch.

On the top, a menu for Mid-County Pizza.

On the bottom: the *Mid-County Inquirer*.

Sanibel Island, Easter 2005

Panorama. The biggest sandcastle on the beach. Sam and the girls worked on it all day, while I brought them shells to shingle the flat roofs, seawater for their moat. As carefully constructed as our home.

Just after spring break, Sam was home for nine nights in a row. The girls acted like it was Christmas. Jamie asked for special menus – steak, turkey, shrimp – and made up place cards every night at dinner. Jordan and Julia argued over who sat next to him and what colour candles we should light. He drove them to their riding lessons on Monday and to dance on Wednesday and he wore his cell phone headset as if he was a rock star instead of a man addicted to voicemail.

'Mommy,' Jordan asked Thursday at breakfast, 'can I take Daddy in for show and tell tomorrow?'

I packed my briefcase while the first pancake burned on the griddle. I stopped and threw it into the disposal, turned down the burner, then made three perfect ones. I told Jordan I didn't think Mrs Wilson wanted humans for show and tell, but things. 'How about the necklace of shells you and I made on vacation? Or that 1930 penny you found when they dug the foundation for the kitchen?'

She poured syrup on her pancakes until the plate was

flooded and countered that the week before, Emily Aharon had brought in her Uncle Mike's purple heart, which happened to be attached to Uncle Mike.

'Well, Daddy doesn't have a purple heart.'

'He has a regular heart,' she said hopefully. 'A good heart.'

I sighed. Why were the fathers always the collector's item? I carried her for nine months, spent twelve hours in labour, and what was her first word? Daddy. I kissed her on the top of her blonde curls and said I thought she'd better think of something else, something she drew or made or collected. Not the Halley's comet appearance of her father.

I took them to school that morning, but Sam picked them up, then worked in the den. When I arrived home at six, Willis was mewing at his bowl and the counter was littered with spent skins of string cheese wrappers. When I opened the garbage to sweep them in, six foil juice pouches were twisted grotesquely on top. The TV upstairs thrummed through the ceiling.

I'll show and tell him, I thought.

The closed den door pulsed with Sam's smooth phone voice. I didn't knock.

'Can I put you on hold a moment?' he asked. He adjusted his headset and raised his eyes at me. 'What?'

'It's dinner-time. They have homework, Sam. They aren't allowed to watch TV during the week.'

'They had a snack,' he countered. 'They said they did their homework already.'

'Did you check it?'

He frowned. 'Check it? My mother never checked my homework.'

'Just because you were deprived doesn't mean—'

'I wasn't deprived, I just wasn't spoiled.'

'Checking homework isn't spoiling them. Letting them drink sixteen ounces of juice before dinner, however—'

He ran his left hand through his hair. The thing he did when he didn't know what else to do.

'I only gave them one juice each.'

'Well, they took another one while you were on the fucking phone.'

'I'm sorry. But I couldn't help it. That was a big call I was on, Claire.'

That's what he says. A big call. A big meeting. Huge.

'Yeah,' I said as I left. 'Little children. Big call.'

Later that night, as I fell asleep to the sound of him tapping on the computer downstairs, when I recall the look on his face when I burst in, a missed detail floated up to me. His face was flushed; droplets of sweat inched down from his sideburns. It matched, in an odd way, the higher tone of his voice as I cut in to his room.

Nervous? Scared? Extortion? Bribery?

Those aren't the things I think. I think phone sex. He was probably having phone sex.

We discover a mutual preference for plain pizza. This works out well given our situation. The newspaper stays on his bed while we go over the rest of the menu. I sense he wants me to ask him for it.

His head leans in, next to mine, as we look over the salads and side dishes. I could head-butt him, I suppose. I could bite his earlobe. Instead I sit. It is warmer with him so close. He smells clean, vaguely citrusy. Or was that just the orange peel still in the trash?

He steps outside to order the pie and a salad. When he comes in, we discuss other foods we like: dark beer, chocolate. Warm tortillas, he says. Raspberries, I say. Avocados.

I know. He smiles.

We could order fajitas next time, I offer.

Maybe, he says quietly.

I am about to ask for the paper when he turns on the television, flips channels. Local news. Sports talk. A movie with Richard Gere dancing.

Do you like to dance? he asks.

Yes, I answer. I think of an old boyfriend who taught me to swing-dance. The thrill of flying into his arms. I dance with my daughters on the weekends, I add.

He turns off the television. What about with your husband?

I shrug. I stop short of telling him how Sam and I used to dance; how I loved the pressure of his hand against my back,

139

the knowing, the guiding, the man-in-charge feeling. If I tell him I like Latin music will we cha-cha on the shag?

Are you a good dancer?

He is taunting me now, eyes two-stepping, asking for it.

I smile. I had stayed long enough with that swing-dancer to learn every move.

I could jitterbug with both hands tied behind my back, I say.

He laughs. You'd have to, he says.

Solid conversations about mindless things. They keep me out of my head. That's what the doctors used to say: Try to stay outside the thoughts. If you can't change them, order them to stop. If they don't stop, rise above them. I imagine all my psychiatrists looking through the opening in the curtains, nodding in approval, as if through the one-way mirror. She is doing better, they will whisper to each other. I think of them as a unit, these doctors from different cities, who heard the same story. They are a kind of family.

He takes the menu back from me. His eyes linger on the Bible on the nightstand.

You are religious? he asks. There is a hint of judgement in the lilt of his voice.

I suddenly fear this discussion: what if he isn't Catholic, but Muslim? Have I misread his ethnicity, his intentions?

I wanted something to read, I say. Like the newspaper.

He fingers it on his bed. I just didn't want to upset you.

Oh, God, I say. The kids? Is something wrong? No one's come, no one's fo—

They have been found.

But are they—

His eyes are soft but serious. They are fine, he says. I just didn't want to make you more nervous than you already are.

He turns away from me, as if he's watching for the pizza delivery.

Give me that paper, I say.

140

The mattress squeaks as he stands up and tosses the paper.

Suit yourself, he says, and walks outside.

Through the window a red Volkswagen Beetle passes, parks. A slice of pizza is painted, orange and yellow, on the door. I don't see the pizza box sliding out of the warming case or the money changing hands. I don't jump up, waving my handcuffs, hoping the pizza boy will understand. I imagine the arrangement: meet me near the office. Not giving out the exact room number.

I unfold the paper.

He comes in with a pizza box and a Styrofoam box of salad.

Eat first, he says.

No, I say.

The lead story: *Three Injured in House Fire*. The photo is a split-level with flames on the roof. There is no crying neighbour or brave fireman or heroic dog in the photo. I feel nothing, looking at it, and am disappointed. When you have only one thing to look at, you want it to be good. I scan the rest of the front page, frowning as I search for my own headline. I expect a minimum of certain verbs and nouns, know better than to expect many adjectives. *Local Woman Thwarts Childnapper*, perhaps. But we haven't made the front page: *Cat Population Soars Across State* has beaten us out.

He eats neatly; his jaw makes little sound. I'm grateful for this. If he gnashed his teeth, snored, or cracked his knuckles it might send me leaping from the window. Sam is quiet too; no talking in his sleep, no yelling at me or the kids. I would rather die in a hail of gunshots than be holed up with a noisy man.

It's hard to enjoy the paper when you can't hold it up in two hands. To turn the page, I have to lay it down flat on the bedspread, then use both hands.

He watches me reading *Deer Wanders Into Graduation Ceremony*, then leans over and takes off my handcuffs.

As I rub my wrists, I find our story: buried, as they say, on

141

page five, in a list of activity by township. Under Creekland Township it says: *Westtown Mother of Three Missing*. At the end of the short, elusive paragraph: 'Her seven-year-old daughter, the only witness, reported the man pulled her mother away in a nightgown.'

I make a face. Was he wearing the nightgown or me? Who the hell edited this?

Did you read this piece of crap? I ask, and he nods. No sign of forced entry? Good God.

I do good work, he replies.

You broke the skylight. You weren't wearing gloves. You had a certain kind of shoes on.

Maybe I had a clean-up crew.

To fix the skylight?

If they had no reason to look on the roof they wouldn't look.

What does that mean?

The police see a certain situation, maybe they make assumptions.

That I'm a bad mother?

That you're an unhappy wife.

I'm not unhappy.

He looks at me oddly. Through me, almost.

Maybe tomorrow's story will be different, he says.

I push the rest of the paper aside: the story about candy-stripers, the recipe for layered salad. He re-ties my hands. I don't need them free to eat the pizza. Mid-County Pizza is the perfect food for imprisoned women. It is pre-cut; no need for risky fork and knife action. The slices are on the small side, ideal for bound wrists.

When we're finished he piles the greasy napkins inside the box and takes it outside. There is a dumpster around the corner; I caught a glimpse of it when we checked in, wondered if he'd be dumping my body there.

The pizza lingers in my mouth; the floury bottom of the

crust, oregano between my teeth. Not unpleasant, not at all. He is gone longer than he needs to be, I think. The dumpster is not that far away. I could get up and hop over to the front window, part the curtain. I could try the bathroom again. I don't. I lie down, full, thinking about the damn paper and the stupid story. Reading the local paper is like reading nothing. An intern probably wrote it. A stringer paid by the hour. My eyes are heavy; I let them fall. I don't hear him come back.

I wake up with a frantic falling spasm. The room is darker than it was before, vaguely orange, like the lamp. Not night, but in between.

He looks at me, breathes deeply.

Are you all right?

I nod.

Your feet were running in the air, like a dreaming puppy.

I flip my thin pillow to the other side, punching it with my hands.

Did he call? I ask.

No answer. He stands up, starts to pace. A bad sign. Men pacing is never something you want to see.

What is Sam waiting for, exactly? A meeting with his accountant? An estimation of my worth?

Did he ask to speak to me? I say suddenly.

Who? he replies.

Sam. Before. Did he ask to hear my voice?

He hesitates and that is my answer.

Why? he finally says. Do you want to talk to him?

Yes, I say.

Really. He raises his eyebrows. Why?

There is something I want out of the house, I say.

He narrows one eye, but doesn't ask.

From my closet, I add.

Do I want him to ask?

He has given me meals, clean clothes, bathroom breaks,

reading material. Of course there are other needs. He would not be surprised by requests for them – water, tampons, Advil, blankets, lip balm, a nail file. More food, different food, things on the side, things that women like. Picky women, needy women, women who cross borders, cut across age, colour, height. Can't live with 'em can't live without 'em women. I want things that aren't available: husband grieving, my daughters' breath on my cheek.

Still, he doesn't ask: he nods. Perhaps when Sam calls back.

When will that be?

He looks at me, says nothing. I see a shrug in his eyes. He doesn't know? Can only guess?

My knees knock together involuntarily. Sometimes the shaking starts in my shoulders, sometimes the knees. When I was thinner, they made more noise. I put my hands to my eyes. As if I can hide from him here.

He walks to the side of my bed. I'm sure he'll call any minute, he says.

I pull my hands away from my face. Try to believe his eyes.

You know, if you use all your energy worrying about the small things, there won't be anything left for the big ones, he says.

I know, I say. I know. Josh and I have had this exact conversation as I watched a clip of a drive-by shooting. If you worry about all the things that *don't* happen to you, Claire, you won't have any energy to fight back when they do.

He walks to his bed, climbs up. He stands at the bottom, clasps his hands behind his back, and swan-dives face forward into his pillow.

Dust billows up from the force of mattress on box spring, and I cough, then burst out laughing.

He smiles, stops short of his giggle. Do it, he says. I'll untie you.

No, no, no.

He pulls me to my feet at the base of my bed. I can't, I protest.

Yes, you can.

He pushes me, his fingers like spiders jumping at the base of my spine. I fly for a second, then put down my hands.

You cheated.

I get back up, sigh.

Trust the pillow, he says.

I'm not worried about the pillow, I say. I'm worried about the headboard.

Close your eyes, then. Just see the pillow in your mind, not the headboard.

As I fall, I feel my hair billowing back, the soft whoosh of my body displacing room 7 air. Flying.

The pillow is a surprise when I land, but a soft one.

You did it. He smiles.

As I climb down I remember the sleepless nights of my childhood, how it all started then. Think of good things, not bad, my father would say.

The pillow not the headboard.

His giggle not his handcuffs.

My freedom, not my ransom.

WEDNESDAY

I used to tell myself no one broke in on a rainy night. That was my small comfort, gleaned from the township police. I called the police chief and used my television credentials, alluding to a story. The statistic he gave me was one of my favourites: even in affluent areas, 95 per cent of break-ins occur on nights without a drop of rain.

There was more I wanted to know: Did they happen most often under a full moon? When it was 80 degrees, not 70, not 90? Were thieves and rapists affected by the wind, the tides, the swelling of the rivers, the migration of birds? Did vagrants travel south for the winter? Were criminals hardened by the same thing that turned the rest of us to stone: 100 per cent humidity?

But all Chief Maloney could tell me was that crime went way up in the summer, and the people who broke windows, kicked down doors, and slid credit cards into jambs preferred not to be wet when they did so. Statistically, what had happened to me was an anomaly: to be abducted during a near hurricane. It was right up there with drag-racing in a blizzard, ransacking a house in the eye of a tornado, bullets hitting you in a hailstorm. The oddity of it, the rareness, was worse than the actual event.

It had taken my mantra away. I couldn't say it any more: *It's raining, I'm safe.* I had to find other comforts, other facts. Had to ignore things I already knew: kidnappings don't usually

end well. Pawns are expendable. Life is short. Men are unpre-
dictable.

We take turns in the bathroom. He goes out, brings back
more Styrofoam cups. Clean clothes wrapped in brown paper.
As I unwrap them with my teeth and one hand, I lean closer,
breathe in the fragrant world outside. No old Cutlass exhaust,
no cargo pockets crammed with oily tools. I crawl inside my
clean clothes and burrow in their artificial floral promise.

I have something else for you, he says.

I look up. Was that shyness I just heard in his voice?
Innocence?

He hands me a rolled-up copy of the *Sentinel*.

My eyes widen.

Not as many stories about cats, he says.

Thank you.

He unties my hands and I open the city paper hungrily
while he checks his voicemail. The national news is relatively
quiet – the disasters all appear to be man-made. A conference
on AIDS is opening in Geneva. More riots in a Paris suburb.
American soldiers still stationed too many places. On the
cover of section two, local news, I am taken aback to see my
own photo: a candid from a cocktail party last year. Black
dress, soft hair, grim expression. Sam would never, never have
given out my picture. Unless he knew David had already
found me? No. No. I run through the possibilities of who
took the picture, who had the picture. Someone who didn't
know better, someone who didn't know I was hiding. I
swallow hard.

The story beneath it is short, but infuriating. At the end is a
quote from Sam, imploring anyone with any information to
step forward. The reporter asks about speculation that I knew
my abductor, and Sam refuses to comment.

Jesus fucking Christ, I say.

Reading the Bible again?

Did you see this? I crumple the paper and gesture in his direction.

I thought it was a better paper.

No sign of forced entry, no evidence of a struggle, and a mention of my lingerie. I struggled!

Yes.

I *did*.

I acknowledge that you did. Yes.

Fucking journalists.

He laughs. Shall I ask them to print a retraction?

Yes, I grimace. And the photo, why such a big photo? That's . . . something a tabloid would do.

He cocks his head. I should think you'd want your picture everywhere. I am the one who should be upset about the photo, not you.

The phone rings and he walks to the door. I feel a small wash of relief. It is impossible for any two people to live together without one of them wanting the other to go. I study the back of his head, the hairline that grows in a V beneath the last wave. The tops of ears that I can't see, the lobes that I can. The left, I note, held an earring once.

As he turns back around, I lower my eyes to the page. On bent knee, he reaches under his bed. Something gold flashes in his left hand, the red-topped screwdriver twirls in his right. The sound of the bit turning into the wood is familiar, comforting. When I look up again, there are two chain locks. Thick like the bracelets boys wore in high school.

He opens the door and covers the phone, whispering: Lock yourself in.

My mouth starts to form a W.

You heard me.

Behind him the sky is darkening. As I hop to the door he watches me through the window, the way you watch a child walk to a distant bathroom. The gold chains sliding, the metal

151

ritual that always calmed me on business trips, gives me no joy. Some kind of necessary risk is being taken. Worth keeping him out to keep out something else.

If he is afraid, what should I be?

I part the curtain with my free hand, watch him walk down the row, past room 9, past room 11. As he reaches the corner, the first wrinkle of lightning cuts the sky above his head, and he jumps. Goosebumps dot my arms beneath the clean T-shirt.

No one breaks in on a rainy night.

Birthday girl, 1968

Square and faded, with a curvy white frame around it. My hair is in pigtails. The package is in tissue paper. I know exactly what's underneath.

My father bought me snow globes from everywhere he travelled. A tradition, one I meant to continue, but didn't. They sat on the shelf overlooking my twin bed and watched over me every night. My soldiers.

My parents owned a small chain of clothing stores, the kind you used to see in malls. They worked late some nights. I rode my bike home after softball or volleyball or cheerleading practice, made myself a sandwich, did my homework, and waited alone with my snow globes. But I was never afraid unless there was a thunderstorm. Outside my picture window the backyard swings swung wildly from the red metal bar. Brown webbed lawn chairs tumbled in cartwheel formation. When I see sprinkling now, that is what I see: not rain, what rain can become.

I don't see the refreshing puddly joy of it. No.

One Saturday morning when Jamie was three and Julia one and a half, they stood at the window and watched the first fat raindrops splatter into a bucket I'd left on the porch. They asked if they could go outside and Sam immediately said yes.

After breakfast, I added. And after you put your toys away.

By the time they finished, and pulled on their boots, the rain had dwindled to nothing. They stood in the backyard, yellow coats and green frog boots, eyes to the now blue sky, waiting for something that would never come. Sam took them by the hand. He walked them underneath the weeping willow tree and told them to close their eyes and count to six. When you hit seven, he said, I promise it will be raining again.

Then he reached up and shook the branches gently. The second-hand rain showered them, and they giggled like they were going through the sprinkler or dancing in the waves. We were all happy then. They were happy to be wet, and I was happy they were safe, in man-made rain, the kind that did not carry the warp of wind or the whip of thunder.

With my hands free, do I untie my ankles, open the door, flag down a passing car?

Do I knot sheets together and lower myself out the bathroom window?

No. I roll into a ball on the bed, grasp my knees like a child, a cannonball grip. Shiver and wait. Shiver and wait. Without my Xanax, I'm at their mercy. I breathe in and out, picture still water, calm water, not rain. When I'm calm, I think, when this passes, I'll consider other action. When I am calm. When this passes.

Then I hear it: I uncurl, sit up with a start. A motel sound, not natural, not rain and wind: TV from the room next door. Through the flimsy wall, the thin headboard, right into my throbbing head.

Like children, TV always sounds louder when it isn't your own. I try to think. The Cutlass did not start up; wherever he has gone is on foot. Did he turn the corner? How far? How long? Long enough to run, to pound on the wall for my new neighbour to help?

I lean into the wall; the TV show could tell me what time it is. I hear a laugh track, then something else, hiding underneath the canned giggles and bright music. The rumble of voices. *In Spanish*.

Scrambling, I go to the opposite wall, put my hand against it. No vibration from the other side of the room. I am not surrounded.

I try to tell myself I'm hearing a Spanish soap opera. *Novelas*. Popular in the Latin community, I'd read about them in a trade publication. I half convince myself there is a thriving Spanish population here in Mid-County.

My heart pounds in my ears with possibility. Is that where he goes when he goes? Next door, talking on the phone to his boss? Never angry, he never needed the television turned up before? But the door, the locks, the warning. No. He went as far as the corner: I watched him go. Someone else is next to me. *Someone is watching?* Someone to lock out?

Someone Spanish. And I had to face it: not David. It was simpler to believe he was coming back to do us in. To finish what he started. But I didn't believe it any more. The years had melted away; maybe his anger had, too. It was time for new, fresh fears.

Next door, the TV goes off. Outside a door snaps open, I sit up, heart pounding. The knock on my door is soft and quick, three in a row, one knuckle.

If I called out 'Who is it?' how would he answer?

I unchain the door.

He walks in swollen and cut, sheepish and dripping wet, a man first, an explanation later.

As he sits down on his bed, I waste no time; I am a mother; I grab a clean towel and run it under cold water. It drips along the shag carpet as I hop over to him. He presses it against his stinging cheek. In the morning there will be bruising and colour. Like anything else it reveals itself later. Right now there is only this. He has taken a kind of bullet. For me.

I sit next to him on his bed.

And I thought *my* boss was tough, I say.

It occurs to me that I have, truly, changed places with my child.

I can't come and go without asking. Someone brings me meals, tells me when to go to the bathroom, when to go to bed.

And now, a grown man stands in front of me and tells me everything is fine, that everything is going to be okay. Never you mind the raised voices behind closed doors, the bruise on the cheek, the eye nearly blackened.

He puts down the towel, walks to the window. The room next door is quiet but I don't trust the quiet.

He paces. His feet move softly, a burglar's gait, but I can still hear the crunching surrender of the nylon shag. I wonder if I had leaned in closer, listened more carefully at the wall, if I could have heard the moment of contact, the crack of knuckle on cheekbone.

Your boss hit you, I say, as if for the record.

He says nothing. I think: I am his bungled deadline, his incomplete report.

He is angry because you took me, I add.

He turns. Looks right at me. His cheek is darker already; the blue coming up through his light brown skin. I remember my daughter's kindergarten question: When black people fall down, what colour are their bruises?

He looks at me and waits. I know the game: he can't tell me, but if I guess right, he will let me know.

I start to play.

157

He is angry because Sam hasn't called back.

He is angry because it's taking too l—

Your husband, he interrupts, is *playing with fire*.

I think of what I expected him to say: Your husband refuses to pay. Your husband asked us to lower the cost by half. Your husband is bargaining for you *like a rug at a bazaar*.

The rain has dwindled to almost nothing now. It doesn't beat against the wooden exterior, but falls, instantly absorbed.

Blood rushes to my face. Embarrassed to be worth so little. What must he think: terrible cook, bad lover, lazy American mother.

It hurts but I know I shouldn't take it personally. Sam is a negotiator by nature. The winning, the small increments that give him even the slightest upper hand, fuel him. Once Hugh, drunk at a cocktail party, told me that Sam loved winning accounts, and hated keeping accounts. And so I was the unusual, the ungettable wife. The infamous, elusive Claire. Got ya now.

Your boss is angry because you are negotiating with Sam?

Let's put it this way: he doesn't agree with how I'm handling the situation.

Our eyes meet. I see the face of a diplomat, a reasonable man hoping for a fair outcome. But he needs more: he needs the upper hand. Sam has to believe he would kill me.

He wants you to cut off my finger and send it to Sam?

No. He pauses. He thinks I should rape you and send him a videotape.

My response surprises even me. I burst into laughter, loud, nervous. The idea is ridiculous, unimaginable.

He smiles despite himself. You would rather I cut off your finger?

No, no, I . . .

You what?

I don't know, I say.

158

His eyes meet mine. If they are saying something in code, I don't know what it is.

A tear falls down my right cheek, then another.

I don't always listen to my boss, he says quietly.

I nod, sniff back more tears.

We can talk about this more tomorrow, before noon, he says.

What's tomorrow at noon?

It is your husband's deadline.

My thumb draws across the gilded edges of the Bible, which is still on my lap. Soft. Much softer than other books. The same way a baby's hairbrush is softer than anyone else's.

Nothing more will happen today, he says quietly.

Is your boss still next door?

He shakes his head. No, he had to meet someone up north.

How can you be sure?

I saw him leave. His car is gone.

He doesn't have a key to this room, or, or, know the owner or anything?

If you are asking whether you are safe—

I nod.

He breathes deeply. You are safe until tomorrow, and then . . .

And then I am not.

He nods slightly in agreement.

The added words don't come off my bitten tongue: And neither are you.

There is something useful in knowing the when of things. It's how people given six months to live feel: they know where they stand, know what they have to do. What if I had known I had only a year to feel safe in my own house? Would I have enjoyed it more, slept better, prepared differently for the hurricane?

And now what? It is afternoon, past lunch, before dinner. How will we celebrate our last night of safety?

He is at the window again. A porthole. He doesn't turn when he talks.

I have a deck of cards, he offers in a faraway voice.

What? I say, unsure.

Cards. Do you want to play cards?

I think of family vacations, the things I packed to keep the girls occupied. The endless games of tic tac toe and Hangman. (One game I do not feel like playing.)

I think long and hard. If he is feeling generous, trying to soothe me, should I let him?

Working mothers have their priorities straight. I know what my last meal should be. Of course I would have a final request: and it is not a round of Crazy Eights.

I want to see my children, I say.

I want to know who David is, he replies.

The seats on the Cutlass are even softer than I remember. Maroon, I see now, and threadbare in places. An interior from another era, gentler than the time I'm in. My hands glide over the seat, erasing the memory of scratchy bedspreads.

He re-ties my hands and feet while we are still in the parking lot. No one sees. Out the window, all of Mid-County is mid-day, mid-work. He and I are the only ones who are mid-kidnapping.

He locks the doors. The electric click of it is something I've imagined in my darkest fears: a miniature prison door. The first time I heard it, it reminded me of David's gun. It doesn't bother me so much now.

We drive. The air-conditioner vents whistle. Outside it is a wet kind of hot. The trees are green, dense from rain. On the edge of the highway, a weeping willow drags against the earth, branch-arms damp and heavy.

He doesn't talk or turn on the radio. Lanes are changed as carefully as they were that first night – Saturday? No, Sunday – using his turn signals. The hope comes back to me: madmen don't use their blinkers.

A few cars join us. It is rush hour in Mid-County. We reach my exit in what feels like an hour, maybe seventy-five minutes.

Get down, he says.

What?

Lie on the seat.

I curl up on the seat and look at the dash.

161

I get carsick sometimes, I warn him.

You'll be fine.

He pulls up to the next light and asks if Sam ever takes the girls to horseback riding.

Dance is Wednesday, I say. Not riding.

I thought it was Thursday.

My stomach churns, imagining the girls' dance calendar crammed into his cargo pocket.

The summer schedule is Wednesday, I say. And then: How did you know?

He shrugs.

You didn't talk to Elizabeth, or—

No.

You're not working with anyone else? No one else knows the girls' schedules?

He turns on his blinker. No.

A few seconds later he asks if Sam ever picks them up at dance.

I breathe deeply. No. He'll probably send his mother.

Wouldn't he be frightened to let them go?

I consider this: Sam scared. Hard to imagine him pacing the floors, jumping at every sound. Will he ever know? Eyes wide, mind racing fear? I want him to. The same way I want him to give birth, to try to braid slippery hair, to prepare three meals and two snacks every day. Try it. See how you like it.

Not with his mother, I say.

I hear the streets of my town pass by, aware that I am separate from where I live. I can't see the movie theatre, the coffee shop, the bakery and ice cream parlour. There are people in each of them, but I don't know any of their names. I hide on the soft velour seat as I have hidden all along.

We idle next to a truck. I hear its huge engine holding itself back with puffs and squeaks. From my angle I can't see the truck driver in the cab but if he wanted to, he could see me. The ropes and reddened wrists, the something-is-wrong-here body inside a driving-suspiciously car. A stranger in a car could take me, and a stranger in a car could save me.

The light turns and we go again. He doesn't turn left into the dance school parking lot, but right. He swings the car around and I get dizzy, spinning, not seeing.

He shifts into park and tells me to sit up.

Out the window, across the busy four-lane street. The tall windows of the dance studio make the girls' pink cheeks and black leotards look even smaller than they are. He opens the glove compartment and hands me a pair of binoculars. What he watched me with. I go in closer: my three daughters are together; they must have blended the two classes for the recital next week. They stand in stair-step order: Jamie, the tallest and darkest, then Julia, smaller but fiercer, and skinny blonde Jordan. Jamie's leotard looks too small for her, I think; it's riding up a little in back. A guilty pang that I hadn't noticed before now. They stand against the pink wallpaper in the corner, near the ballet barre, giggling. As they jeté across the floor, toward the window, I can tell they are off beat, hearing some other music in their head. I watch them bob and sway, and they do not see me. It is what parenting is, the whole equation. The children watched and the parent invisible.

He doesn't look down at his hands, or nervously out the Cutlass window. He watches too. He doesn't ask me which ones are mine. He is not another parent in the audience. Still, his face is placid, patient, a smile threatening at the corners of his mouth. It is the face of a father. Now or some day. Men who love children live differently in the world. They smile at smeared faces in restaurants, watch ball games at playgrounds, wave back to the little hands in station wagon windows.

Latin paramedic child-loving hitch-knot-tying once had an earring kidnapper of mine.

What's your name?

He hesitates, but doesn't smile.

You know my name, it's only fair.

I don't have a name, he says, looking back at the dancers.

At the end of the song, they are supposed to finish with a stag leap. As I watch Jamie's legs propel off the ground, thin and strong as a racehorse's, it is impossible to imagine them bound with rope, quivering in a motel room. We are both meant to be where we are. The teacher applauds, then crosses the room to put a hand on her shoulder, leans down and smiles. A kindness for the girl who was nearly kidnapped and couldn't save her mother.

In the parking lot below the window, my mother-in-law's silver sedan pulls in. The licence plate gives her away: *Brdwtcr*. She stays in her car, facing forward, missing the rarest sightings of them all.

The lesson ends and most of the girls rush to gather their street shoes, at the other end of the studio. Jamie walks to the window. She puts her hand over her eyes and looks straight across at the Cutlass. After I was dragged away did she go to the window and watch us drive away? Had she seen him before, idling behind the wheel?

No, she is just looking into the window like a mirror. Posing, pouting, testing a more grown-up version of herself.

Jamie, I mouth. Oh, honey.

He looks at me and does not need to say it. I lie down on the seat. As we drive in the opposite direction I remember a composition they sometimes dance to: Bach. My heartbeat catches up to it, keeping time.

I think I'm going to call you Jose, I say.

He snickers. That's not very original.

As we pull further and further away, I want to say thank you. Thank you, Jose. But I don't.

I know why he brought me to the parking lot.

I owe him now.

Hawaii, June 1996 The honeymoon suite

Sam is drunk in the picture; he has that loopy smile. We went to Hawaii because it was one place neither of us had ever been.

It was a long trip, the last leg in a minibus that pitched up the cliffs, leaned around the lush green switchbacks. We slept late, then walked, bought postcards and beach chairs, and when it started to drizzle, we did the only sensible thing: went to a local bar. It looked like a shanty, someone's small but proud home, rocking chairs on the porch. Sam saw the Budweiser clock glowing through the window, or we would have passed it. The three men at the bar were drinking beer but a small chalkboard offered margaritas. The blender beckoned, and we were smashed, giddily smashed, within the hour.

We sat and laughed on the porch, our pitcher of margaritas like a third guest at the table, as the wet tourists paraded by on the street, wringing out their guidebooks, holding heavy towels above their heads. We were drunk-dry, I said, and Sam laughed. In the beginning, he always laughed at my jokes, my small turns of phrase. He pulled a piece of beach glass from his pocket and gave it to me.

When it was time to leave, we realized our traveller's cheques were back in the room; we only had change left from the twenty we'd broken for postcards. I counted twice to be

165

sure: fourteen dollars. The bar bill, without tip, was twenty-four.

'Give him your watch,' I giggled to Sam.

'I tell you what,' the bartender countered. 'If you kiss me, we'll call it even.'

I burst out laughing, then realized he was dead serious.

'Ten dollars for a kiss? Not bad.' Sam shrugged. 'At that rate you can quit your job.'

The other men snickered with Sam. I laughed too, at first. Then I realized how soberly the bartender was looking at me.

He could have been forty, possibly more. He was deeply tanned, his face lined, but his lips didn't have that salty surfer look. His hair faded from brown all the way to golden blond on the tips. If I could live with a man like David, couldn't I love that beach hair for a few seconds?

I stood up. He was a good height. I leaned in and closed my eyes, all lips, no hands, no hips. His right hand touched my hair lightly, guiding me.

The air around me was full of him, not Sam. I waited for my husband's hand on my wrist, the intervention of arm, the protest of voice. But Sam did not move. I felt him not moving. Just watching.

The bartender tasted of coconut. He didn't take the full ten dollars worth, didn't push it. It was like a good first kiss on a doorstep. When he pulled away I tried hard not to smile.

I don't know what Sam saw in that moment: everything he feared or everything he wanted. If someone had taken a photograph of that evening before we got home, snapped it in time, I would have been the carefree one in it. Devil may care. Sold a kiss for a tenner. What a pistol.

But now I see the lack of movement in it, the non, the un. And I see Sam whistling as we made our way home along the dirt road, leaning drunkenly into the wind, while we both struggled to keep our footing at the edge of the slippery grass.

At dusk the light is turning again, orange and pink, hot before the cool of night. We are back on the road everyone calls a throughway. It has a number but no one remembers it. Here, things are referred to in the past tense. Go to the old post office. Turn on the old access road. Drive past the abandoned stables. Stay right at the fork by what used to be Miller's Farm. The road curves gently and offers little shoulder, like old roads used to.

When I hear it, at first, I think nothing of it. A sound effect. What comes down a country road now and then. It doesn't stand out in the landscape of wind, tyres, brakes, trucks changing gears. What stands out are Jose's eyes darting in the rearview mirror. His shoulders stiffening.

The siren grows louder and I understand.

Gaining on us. More than one? I turn my head, see flashing light in the distance.

He speeds up just slightly and speaks without turning his head.

Climb into the backseat and pull the tab on the armrest.

What? I say.

Go.

Why?

It opens to the trunk.

I freeze. The sirens wail now.

Do it! he barks.

The fear in my head is my own siren.

I can't, I cry. I can't go in there, I'm—

Get in now!

No, I—

Listen to me, he yells, trying to outrun the sirens. You do *not* want me to use the gun in my pocket. You'll be safe in the trunk. Now go!

I climb into the backseat awkwardly, restricted by ropes and sobs. With my teeth, I pull the tab that opens into the cave of the trunk. It reeks of gas and oil.

I cry out.

I turn, see Jose's eyes in the rear-view mirror. They are softer than they were a moment ago.

It will only be for a minute, Claire. I promise.

The first time he has used my name.

We are both on a first-name basis now.

I hold my breath and start to scoot in. The opening snaps shut on a spring as if rigged. It is so cold and dark it feels wet. My feet touch metal and I pull away. I imagine the worst: gasoline, oil. Soaking my cotton clothes like the wick of a lamp. My whole body shakes, my knees and teeth banging together with every indentation or swell in the road. I am a human Molotov cocktail, rolling into trouble, waiting, just waiting to blow.

If you doubt the thinness of metal, ride in a trunk for a few miles. It is skin, not armour. You hear the wind, the trucks, the sirens. You feel the air through the cracks and seams. It's the closest you'll ever get to being a cheap machine.

I put my head in my hands, cover my eyes, and tell myself that is why it is dark. I'm just covering my eyes, I think. I breathe in and out slowly. I'm in a womb, not a trunk. In a bed, not a trunk.

We slow down. I hear gravel beneath the tyres, then a gripping, a stop.

The siren is gone and I listen for footsteps, cop-crunch. I

168

wait for gunshots. There is nothing. A car door opens, closes. I can't tell from where. I keep my head in my hands. My brain starts to shuffle, to analyze the possibilities. On my list, all the worst things come first. He will leave me in here. He will push the car over a cliff. He will— Stop, my mouth moves. I pinch the inside of my wrist. Stop.

As the trunk swings open from the inside, not the outside.

You can come out now, Jose says.

He pulls my wrists with both hands and in a minute I'm in the backseat. He looks me over, inspecting for damage. There is none. I survived. I was in the trunk, now I'm in the seat. It is astonishing to me, and perhaps to him. It's after, and I'm no different. The before, the quaking, quivering before, seems far away.

They weren't after us. Three of them, he adds.

I nod. Good for him, bad for me.

We get in the front seat and he turns the key.

We probably shouldn't have left the room, he says, stating the obvious.

But, he adds as he merges, they haven't traced the licence plate number.

I knew it wasn't your car, I reply.

His smile broadens. You picture me in a more stylish car?

Yeah, try stealing something newer next time.

Ah, I forgot about you and the tyres. He pumps the brakes twice to make them squeal and I shriek.

Jose's laugh is boyish again, and it feels like a reward for being in the trunk. French fries, bubble bath, laugh.

David and his other girlfriend, 1989

He said he bought the car to match my eyes, but it was never mine. He loved that ancient pale turquoise Karmann Ghia more than me. He loved a few things more than me, as it turned out. And he came after them with a fury, even after we got back to the States and I rented the townhouse with Jesse. I still remember the familiar shape of that car, the friendly headlights turning into a menacing face as it appeared in my rear-view mirror.

How many days did he follow me before he found out where I lived? Three, four? I'd manage to shake him twice by driving towards the police station. But he kept coming back and finally I realized he knew where I worked. There just weren't that many places a television news writer could ply her trade. He found the station, in the very first town where I sought refuge. Dead roses arrived at my desk one morning, and I knew. As I threw them away my cheek burned with the memory of the last time I'd seen him, the imprint always there of his knuckles against bone.

He followed me from the station, over and over, nearly running me into a ditch one time. I should have let him, I know that now. It would have been getting off easy.

Later that night, at two or at three, when I dream of him grabbing me, I don't know who it is at first. It's hazy, that place between asleep and awake. But it doesn't hurt. His angry nails, scratching, don't draw blood, lift skin. When I dream of my head hitting the thin headboard it doesn't ache, swell like an egg, break open, bleed. The scratchy bedspread does not scratch in my dream. My bare back, thrown against it, doesn't rub raw. The corner of it stuffed in my mouth is nothing. The gag does not make me gag in the least.

When I dream of the orange glazed lamp knocked over in the frenzy, it doesn't break, but falls away harmlessly, like candy glass. His fingers on my throat look menacing, but feel innocent.

The sounds, the images, all in place.

When I dream of him raping me it is not rape. His hands tear at me, claw and rake, hard bone, sharp shovel, soft touch. Every throw and toss, head whipped back, angry thrust and parry, beat crunch grind is tender light sweet.

He ruins me without paining me.

I turn to the camera and pretend he is hurting me, acting, conjuring, calling forth the blood and bruises.

Letting Sam see what he wants to.

It is my dream.

It is our game.

First day of school, 2005

Julia's cheeks are as bright as her red backpack. She came
home excited about everything, her desk, her subjects, all she
would learn. Her Spanish teacher had taught her to count to
five already! At dinner-time Sam called from wherever he was
– Santa Fe? Santa Ana? – and spoke to each girl about her
day. I stood at the stove and listened to one side of the
conversation; they were just recounting everything they'd
already told me. Jamie was happy with her new classroom,
which was conveniently located between the library and the
gym. Jordan, still in Pre-K, was relieved to discover that the
boys had a separate bathroom. And Julia was just thrilled
that she could speak a language her little sister couldn't.
'*Pinata*!' I heard her say through the phone. '*Blanca*!'

They hung up before I could speak to Sam; I thought about
calling him back but the oven timer went off and the potatoes
started to boil over and I forgot what I wanted or needed to
say. I knew he'd call later to say goodnight.

Later, as I tucked Jordan in, she told me that on the phone
Daddy said, 'Tell all my girls I love them,' and she asked,
'Even Mommy?' and he said, 'Of course, Mommy is a girl.'

'Yes.' I smile. 'We're all girls here.'

That night, like so many, I couldn't sleep: I swore I heard
whispering in the house. I made the round of the girls' rooms

to see who was talking in their sleep. Usually I'd write down what they said and in the morning, we'd all laugh at how it didn't make sense. 'I said what about the monkeys, Mommy? Tell me again!' When Sam was gone we kept a little book so we could tell him all the sleep-talking tales he'd missed. I found it once in his briefcase; he stole it to take on his trip.

But the girls' rooms were silent, except for their breathing. In the hallway I heard the whispering coming from downstairs.

I ran to the window; Sam's car was next to mine. He was due back in the morning and it was technically that. I walked down the stairs. His back was to me, our phone, not his, in one hand.

I squinted as if it would help me hear, help me understand the words that were coming out of his mouth. '*Sí, sí. Por favor. Alliente.*'

Yes. Please. Hurry.

I went back to bed without asking what he was doing, what he meant, who he was calling. It's easy to say that I should have. It's not that it didn't register, that I didn't process it. I did.

I went to bed and thought, Good. He can help Julia with her Spanish.

THURSDAY

My eyes open. Three blinks before I say it: Today's the day. Good or bad, today. The wedding day sentence doesn't differ much from the electric chair sentence. Knowing is knowing. The impulsive don't know this pleasure. Today I'll walk down the aisle. Today I'll jump off a bridge.

The need to know has almost consumed me at times. Investigative reporting at work and at home. A battle against secrets, whispers, bumps in the night. All my fears, obsessions, addictions, centred around the need to know. People like me become journalists, therapists, detectives, archaeologists. Together we dig through the evidence, sift answers from dust. Try fail try fail try fail. Less satisfying than it is necessary. I was always obsessive, the doctors said. Always. As if that should comfort me.

I roll over. Jose's bed is smooth, made. Alone again. The sun fights the thin curtain; if I stood up and went to the window, felt the fabric, it would be warm. I don't. I rub my eyes and sit up.

Today's the day.

Is Sam waking up somewhere, saying this too?

When he first started travelling, about a year into our marriage, he'd call me from the hotel room and leave a message: I'm looking at the moon. Are you looking at the moon? And I'd call him back, leave word at the desk: Tell the gentleman in room 309 that I'm looking at the moon. Is he looking at the

179

moon? And so it would go, on and off. I'm going to bed at ten, are you going to bed at ten? I'm eating a mint from my pillow, are you eating a mint from your pillow? Now I can't remember how it ended; who said what the last time.

Outside I hear a car; different than the Cutlass. I hop to the window, open the curtain another inch, look left. The glass seems wavy, as if from the heat. The Cutlass is not in its space. On the right, a green car leaves the parking lot. An Accord, I think, with a woman so short behind the wheel I can't imagine how she can see. My only chance to flag down a car, gone.

When I turn to go, something catches my eye.

The sun sparkles on the new metal of the door, shinier, bright yellow: a keyed deadbolt. I narrow my eyes, go back slowly to the wavy glass. It looks different, another layer, a sturdy storm window layered inside. Something. Around the frame the caulk is toothpaste-bright and expertly straight, as if he used a level. When I touch it, it leaves powder on my finger.

I suck in my breath, go to the bathroom window. A set of iron bars affixed inside, blocking entry.

Deadbolts, bars. And the glass . . . bulletproof? Clearly Jose installed them while I slept. I wonder where on earth he could have bought them, who else he had to bribe. Or . . . did he have them already, an inventory?

Is he using them to keep me in, or keep someone else out? I consider the lack of housekeeper, night manager, occupants. Does Jose's boss own the motel?

The need to know comes over me like a wave. You call it courage; the doctors call it compulsion. I dive under my bed for the videotape.

The VCR is close enough to the window that I think I'll hear him pull up. I turn it on, slide the tape in, sit down on his taut bed. I expect to see myself or Sam, but hope for more. There is no reason to watch my own surveillance. I'm not that bored or that vain.

In the beginning of the tape, there is nothing but black. Ten seconds at least, enough scratches that I know I'm on the right channel. When the picture comes on it doesn't explode. Not shocking, not loud. No torture or porn, the collection of another man. There is a building, a corridor, a cramped laboratory. Dozens of women toiling, shirts damp at their bent backs. There are closed windows and high ceilings. Portable burners, glass containers. An assembly line of sorts, but the product is not apparent. I squint, as if it will make something clear to me. But nothing about the space, the women, the work they are doing, tells me what year it is or what they are making. The women all have dark hair; some have dark skin.

Suddenly a shiver creeps up my spine. Not from the tape. My eyes travel slowly to the right. Jose's face is there, in the crack in the curtain. In the next second the deadbolt is open and his finger is on eject.

I scramble to get off his bed. Away. The last thing I see on the tape is an opening, an escape, a porthole.

High above the lab, when the camera pulls back, a plastic skylight.

Closed.

From Jose's pocket, a padlock. He grabs the tape, scrambles beneath his bed and counts in Spanish under his breath. The lock clicks and spins. He stands up and looks at me. My eyes avert, ashamed, caught with his things.

I'm sorry, I cry. But I don't under—

You don't understand? You aren't supposed to understand! You are supposed to sit and wait and . . . He takes a deep breath. And serve your *purpose*, he finally spits out.

I look at him: his face doesn't match his words. Is he just repeating what someone else said?

If you explain what's going on, I say quietly, I could help you negotiate with Sam.

From his other pocket, he pulls a newspaper, throws it on the bed. I look up at him, and see what he doesn't say: I bring you the paper, and this is the thanks I get?

He licks the corner of his lip, exhales loudly.

You want me to explain?

I nod.

Okay. I'll explain if you agree to two conditions.

Which are?

One, no matter what happens, you will not tell my boss what I have told you. Two . . . you will tell me who the hell David is.

I blink. Those are his terms. We have to trust each other with our stories.

Okay, I say quietly.

He sits on his bed and looks at his hands.

Have you ever heard, he begins, that some prescription drugs are much cheaper in Mexico? Cheaper even than Canada?

I have a friend who always buys Renova on vacation, I say.

There are a lot of people like your friend. People who come to Mexican pharmacies. People who buy off the internet from Mexican companies. Or Canadian or British too.

Yes.

There is a great demand for certain drugs. Certain American-made drugs.

I feel the webby beginnings of something coming together. Drugs, pharmacies, pharmaceutical companies, corporate retreats, round-table discussions, marketing strategies, international travel, husband never home. The threads start to feel tighter around my neck. I tug at the collar of my cotton shirt.

The pharmacies and the pharmaceutical companies are losing money every time a tourist buys a drug in Mexico. Unless . . . they have manufactured that drug in Mexico.

I nod. It all rings true so far.

So someone had the brilliant idea to set up Mexican labs.

I frown. This sounded like the argument I made to Michael about family-run furniture factories in the central part of the state. I'd heard from a decorator about getting cabinetry at cost. I'd spoken to an ER nurse who told me about seven-year-old boys coming in with sliced-off fingers. I was learning about Amish rites of passage for young boys. Michael had said: *Claire, you are the only person I know who puts two and two together and gets nine.*

I brush him off in much the same way Michael brushed me off.

Manufacturers use foreign suppliers all the time, I say.

These are unregulated labs. The conditions are terrible, there is no ventilation—

Sweatshops?

Yes. In Mexico we call them *maquiladoras*. Everywhere in the *barrio*, there are *maquilas*.

I nod. I remember learning about factory life in Mexico City when I researched the Pakistani factories.

I've done stories on the garment industry. Overseas, I say.

He nods. There is one important difference, he says. Between this and that.

Which is?

The fumes from drugs kill you a lot faster than the fumes from dyes and cloth.

My breath catches in my chest. I would be quick to blame Sam for almost anything, but death? I rub my collar bone, my heart. Is this real fear? This red cave I'm falling into between my bones?

How many? I ask quietly.

Four hundred women and children in the last two years. Girls as young as eleven.

Why hasn't anyone heard about this?

Maybe because there are no Latino producers on *60 Minutes*.

Can't the government regulate it?

The government . . . is paid off by someone we both know.

My hand goes from chest to mouth. No. I think of the shiny photos from Sam's trips: oceans, mountains, deserts, orange streaky skies. Golf clubs, skis, rods and reels shipped ahead to his destinations. When he called the girls on his cell phone, there was always laughter in the background. At home, it rained and the basement flooded; the cat box spilled and the toilets overflowed and the car alarm went off. And Sam always came home tan. No lipstick on his collar, but too much colour in his cheeks. One spring we posed for a family portrait and I told him he looked like he came from a different country. Claire, he said, don't be jealous just because you miss travelling for your job.

He fished in Mexico, I say dumbly.

The three biggest American pharmaceutical companies employ your husband to run interference for them. To do whatever needs to be done. Which does *not* include fishing, Jose says.

I breathe in deeply. Sam had pharma clients, I knew this. And he had been to Mexico several times that I knew of. But I remember more now: the FedEx packages, the phone calls. Even changing cooking habits. Since when do you like chilli peppers? I'd asked him the week before.

Okay. Let's say you're right. Why go after Sam? Why not the heads of the companies? They're the ones with the deep pockets.

Because, he said quietly, they are not the ones with the dirty hands. They are not the ones who went to the police and the villages and made it all happen.

So I'm here because Sam gave money to corrupt policemen?

You are here, he says sharply, because he gave the people of Mexico City false hope! He had his people round up a few *señoritas* with sparkling jewellery and sent them into the *barrios* to talk about all the money to be made! *Forget the other maquiladoras, they pay nothing, come work for us!* Come to our factory and die! That's what your husband was doing in Mexico! Fishing for victims!

I bite my lip, look away, ashamed of my own stupidity. I'm not the kind of woman who knows nothing. I'm not the kind of woman who discovers gambling debts, foreign bank accounts, shady offshore corporations.

What about Sam's partners? I ask. Is Hugh involved? Anne? I picture them kidnapped, too. Held captive in room 11 or 13.

I don't know how much his partners know.

How can you be sure that Sa—

My boss has proof. We have informants. We have tapes.

The math sinks into my skin: what is one woman dead in the

face of four hundred? It is nothing personal. But Jose's anger, his righteousness. How is that not personal?

How will this stop the other companies, how—

Is there anything more frightening to a rich American than a series of kidnappings?

Series? My eyes widen.

Sometimes, he says softly, people don't hear you the first time. He clears his throat. It's your turn – he starts to say.

I bite the corner of my lip. Where to begin?

 – your turn to shower. He nods toward the bathroom.

He unties my feet and I go in, close the door. My clothes are wrapped in brown paper on the toilet seat. There is an empty paper bag on the floor for the ones I'm wearing. This is Jose's life now, these errands of ours. Laundromat, coffee shop, diner, news-stand. I brush my teeth and turn on the shower, step in, try to wash away my confusion. Would my husband do anything for a client, even let women die? Then it slips in: Today. *I* could die today. Four hundred and one.

I squat in the shower, sobbing, hand over mouth. I cry until there is nothing left but the blame. It burns in my rib cage, an angry husk, a car fire on the side of the road. Every man is capable of hurting a woman and Sam was no different. But four hundred women and children?

His soft knock interrupts me.

Are you almost done? he calls.

Yes, I choke back.

I turn the shower off, dry body, tears. The sound of his voice is soft again.

I walk out and look Jose in the eye.

You realize I could also die today, I sniff.

At least – his eyes twinkle – I have given you clean underwear.

On my nightstand there is an orange lamp, black tea, toast and the paper folded to the crossword puzzle. I sit down.

At the window, Jose clicks his phone shut, turns.

Sam's secretary, he says.

There is a tone in his voice somewhere between mockery and derision.

I lift an eyebrow while I sip my tea. I'm trying to stay cool, not let on that I don't like her and her straight blonde hair, don't trust her, don't want her relaying messages about my life. Mel-a-nie. I even hate her name.

He's calling at eleven thirty, he adds.

I nod. The call before the call. A classic Sam move. When Jamie was a toddler, Melanie would call at seven and say Sam would be calling to say goodnight at eight. Clanking dishes, changing diapers, knee-deep in toys, I would drop everything to answer the phone, and it would be the call before the call, and not the call. Sam blamed Melanie and her attention to running his calendar, his day, his week. To keeping him on schedule, like a gynaecologist. He was also known for the meeting before the meeting. Hugh told me: Sam always made a point of 'popping his head' into someone's office on his way to the conference room. He would pretend to be lost, looking for the restroom, then happen past the executive's suite. The best way to drop a hint, make a singular point: one on one, before the meeting.

He watches me as I eat my toast, hoping for more, or knowing more, I don't know which. I say nothing. I feel his eyes linger, digging. I have the feeling I sometimes get with a new acquaintance – just after they have offered the first secret, a titbit, from their past. They serve it to me, then wait, hoping I'll reciprocate. There are other people, I know, who see them in me: dark secrets, shadows swimming just below my surface. They rise up now and then, flashing, threatening to show like a bruise. I know Jose sees them, and soon he will ask for a closer look. The story I owe him.

For now, I offer nothing. I eat my toast and unfold the *Sentinel*.

Anything new in the investigation?

He shrugs.

No strands of your hair, no licence plate number from the neighbours?

It's not the *New York Times*.

Meaning?

A small smile threatens at the corners of his mouth. They could have made a mistake, he says.

Today's top story is *Heat Wave Cripples State-wide Power Stations*. There are tornadoes in Tulsa. Wildfires in California. Rioters at the AIDS conference in Geneva. One day, and all hell has broken loose.

I scan through the front section until I see it: *New Details Emerge in Westtown Kidnapping*. I read the two paragraphs and look at Jose accusingly.

I didn't write it, he says.

Jamie said she'd seen you somewhere before? I spit through my teeth. Did you follow my daughter? Were you near my house, in my yard, *before* that night?

No.

I kick the paper off the bed.

It's not that bad.

Oh no? What about the part that says, 'This adds to the growing belief that she knew her alleged abductor'?

190

It's harmless.

No, it isn't. Because my husband will think, my daughters will think. My breath catches in my chest.

Will think what?

That I left them for you, I whisper.

Sam knows that's not the case.

Does he? How could he? I ask, tears filling my eyes. When there's that other piece of crap reporting? The description of you as medium height, well-built, toffee-coloured skin?

You find this inaccurate?

I laugh, sniff the tears back. Good God. Jamie could not have used those words. If they have another witness they aren't named in the article. They're as unprofessional as the *Mid-County Inquirer*.

Perhaps it is Sam that coached her, that emphasized this.

What?

Well, you leaving with a man you may have known . . . it points far away from his business, doesn't it?

I blink. Jesus, I say.

Isn't this what your husband really does for a living? Manipulates the truth for his big clients?

You don't know him. He's not—

Not what?

Evil, I say. He's not evil. I pick at my dry cuticles.

You think one person can truly know what is in another's heart?

I look up. His eyes meet mine and hold. They are dark, almost black, with no glints of caramel or gold, no light. But they are deep, and they don't look away or narrow when a subject cuts.

Yes, I say.

He nods and twists his mouth in a way I haven't gotten used to, and can't decide if I like.

191

You think that is what marriage is about, knowing every-thing?

Not knowing *everything*, I say. But knowing the essential, I suppose. The core.

Some people believe in the mystery of the other person.

I shake my head. Not me.

Okay, okay. We disagree. He gathers the paper from the floor. Maybe you shouldn't read the paper any more.

Just give me the crossword, I sigh.

Local crosswords are a good barometer of a place. This one is easier than usual, full of puns and references to pop culture. No classic literature, no history, no foreign phrases. It's just as well; I'm out of practice. A few words in, I'm stumped. Actor Jane? Jane Fonda? One letter too short. Jayne Meadows? One letter too long and I'm certain there is that 'y' in her first name. He sees me squinting and comes over to look. His head is so close I smell lime.

Maybe they mean author Jane, I say. Jane Austen, Jane Smiley. They both fit. Jane Fonda and Jayne Meadows don't.

It says actor, not actress.

No, actor is generic now. It's used for both.

Maybe not here.

I shrug. It is a reasonable point: we are mid-county after all.

Don't know any men named Jane. Carroll, yes. Robin, yes. But—

Could it be a last name?

I blink. Thomas Jane. It fits. I pencil it in.

I hate you, Jose. I say.

He laughs, gets off the bed.

My wife used to say, 'It's not a vocabulary test, it's a game.'

I look up. Here it is again: the tit looking for a tat. He will want a fact in return.

You have a wife?

I did.

192

Oh.

You seem surprised any woman would have me. He smiles.

No. You seem unmarried. Younger than me. I . . . just assumed.

I am older than you think.

I consider this. It's an interesting combination, lightness with heft. A college professor or war vet. The oldest orphan of six. Someone who had to get it together early.

You were a paramedic in the Gulf War, I blurt out.

He blinks twice.

You went to school here, that's how you know English, then you went to Desert Storm and sent part of your pay cheque to your mother and siblings in Mexico.

I'm part of your puzzle now? he asks.

I look down, embarrassed.

This is how journalists work, with wild guesses?

I know you work in health care, I say.

He exhales and looks away. You are right, he says finally. I was an orderly at a bilingual hospital. I learned English at night. Does that make you happy?

Yes.

You don't know everything, he says, and goes outside.

The deadbolt locks and the Cutlass beckons. I don't see him after that, but I imagine him on the phone, talking to his boss, filling him in. I don't know what time it is, but I hazard a guess: ten o'clock.

I finish my tea and try to finish my puzzle. I can't for the life of me remember the name of Elaine's boyfriend on *Seinfeld*. A few letters fill in, and finally I get it: Puddy. It takes me longer than usual, but all the squares are filled in. An accomplishment. I do them every morning over coffee at my desk, or in the pre-sunrise hour before the girls get up. Sometimes it is the only thing I get right all day.

I open the drawer and take out the Bible, flip through. So

much of it is foreign to me, the language, the stories. There is comfort in here somewhere; another person could turn to it. I wrinkle my nose at the formal phrasing, the shalt nots, as unfamiliar as Shakespeare. I dropped history out of my life in college. Stopped looking back and started looking forward. Fearing what was about to happen instead of what already had.

On the other side of the wall, a phone screams and I jump.

The Spanish voice speaks quickly, rising in intensity. It begins to sound like an argument. I move slowly away from the wall, toward the window, and pull the curtain back. Outside Jose is on the phone, gesturing, chopping the air. I feel sick to my stomach: are they speaking to each other, arguing about me? No; there must be a third person. A three-way call, and all of them furious.

The voice stops next door. Outside Jose clicks his phone shut. Yes. Not coincidence, fact. I drop the curtain, step back toward the bed. The air conditioning comes on loudly: a language I understand.

A door opens, then a yelp comes from the room next door: vicious and hyena high; the door slams again. I throw the curtain open, fearing for Jose.

He is headed to our room, eyes down, hand over his mouth. Defeated.

Fear chimes in my chest, striking twelve.

I reach up to the chain locks, fumbling, trying to save myself from his bad news.

Too late.

He is quicker than I am again.

How is it I never know a man is going to hurt me until he does?

Some women have better radar than others. They see shifty eyes instead of bedroom eyes, sense a hug turning into a trap. Not me: I've spent a decade fearing the imagined men. Nothing left over for the man standing in front of me.

Was Jose's lip quivering as he backed me on to the bed? Or did I just wish it was?

He ties my hands and feet more quickly than before. The bandanna he pulls from his pocket is roughly new, unwashed. It scratches as he wraps it across my eyes, ties it almost too tight.

He fumbles beneath the bed.

Drink this, he says.

Poison? It is almost a whimper.

Vodka, he replies.

What?

Just do it.

He lifts a pint to my lips. The liquid burns: cheap vodka. I know the difference.

More, he says.

I drink, but not quickly enough. It leaves a sticky trail down my chin. Does the vodka numb my cheek, deaden it when his fist slams into it the first time? No. Do alcohol and blood mixed in your mouth taste any better than blood alone? Not especially.

He hits me once on each side of my face. One, two. Both are

a bone-rattling surprise. That he would do it at all. That he would do it again. Finally I am intelligent enough to wince for a third, but it doesn't come.

The tears on my cheeks burn. The Polaroid camera makes a party sound. I half expect to hear the pop of balloons or champagne. I've never associated this camera with the possibility of snuff movies, police work, kidnapping evidence. He takes two shots. One, two. The camera goes back under the bed.

You said you wouldn't hurt me, I say. My voice is small, barely making it through my cowering torso. I remember my dream, how he didn't hurt me in it, how I couldn't imagine it.

He says nothing, goes to the bathroom, runs water. I hear him speaking Spanish: *Perdonar.*

It sounds like French: Forgive me.

I do not for one second believe he is talking to me.

My eyes close and the swelling begins. The lid grows and throbs, distorting the image beneath it: a blurry portrait of Sam, the man I married who'd never fought in a bar, wouldn't dream of spanking our daughters, and ferried spiders from house to yard in one cupped hand.

June 1996, Nantucket First Bay Church

Dark print, low light in the vestibule. I pace inside the panelled room in my ivory dress, the only white relief in the shot. Even in profile, you can see worry in the lines of my jaw. Sam, late for everything, predictably holding up his own wedding.

It was cute at first, the way he always ran in, hair flying, arriving with embroidered apologies. It was clients, always the siren call of a client. Most jobs divide people in two: the workplace battling the home for priority. Sam was splintered in all directions. He was a pie chart, carved up by each client. He would do anything, apparently, for a client. Travel everywhere. Take phone calls in the middle of anything. At community parks, at hospitals, in school gymnasiums, there are people talking to their families, and there is always one man who stands apart, talking urgently into his phone. Sam is that man.

We talk of living in the moment; I believe Sam lives in other people's moments, their calls and needs drawing him in, the smiling happy-go-lucky person in the background of all your pictures. The photos in the business section, the ribbons being cut, the jumbo cheques handed out; Sam is on the edge of them all; the person who starts to look familiar even if you don't know who he is. In all the pictures I have of him, bundled with a rubber band in the box, he is ready. Cocked head full of floppy hair, white teeth, happy to oblige.

And I wonder, if Sam and I were switched, and he was the one beaten in room number 7, if the sound of the Polaroid grinding into action would automatically produce a bloody grin. Reflexive, instinctive, like blinking or breathing to another man.

Jose leaves me on the bed with a wet motel hand towel and walks out the door, wordlessly. Against my cheek, the raised letters on the white towel speak too loudly: the M-I-D, then the dash before County, rub raw. I take turns shifting the cold letters to the other cheek. I think of Luke, who tried to comfort me after my father's funeral, how tentative and small his arms were, how they didn't reach all the way around.

These are my comforts: I think of the men in my life, and wonder which one might have saved me, might have done all the right things in the right order. Which one would not have travelled on a business trip, would not have done what his client asked, would not have said anything to a kidnapper but where? And how much? My father, yes. Anyone else? When I retrace Sam's steps in other men's shoes, they lead in a variety of directions: to a tent, not a house. To children who are boys, not girls. To Paris. To prison. To a hospital. Worse places, not necessarily better. But not to the room that I'm in. No. This is where Sam and I have ended up.

Your husband is playing with fire. Maybe your husband is pointing the investigation away from his business. Is that what is happening? Or what he wants me to think?

Sam bribing officials, dazzling the local girls. I'd seen him discreetly tipping maître d's, and winning over entire convention halls with his speeches. Were these all the same skills? Was charm just manipulation with a smile?

Too much thinking; my head throbs. I hear blood rushing from the bruises through my temples, and am terrified, suddenly, that my head will burst. His punch lit a fuse; it leads to an aneurysm or stroke. I am about to explode.

No, I whisper, as tears burn through my blindfold, and sting my scraped cheeks. Stop. Stop.

Soon Sam will have the Polaroid, then the police, then the paper. The world will think they know something I don't. Criminal/victim. Devil/angel. Monster/damsel. They won't see the shading in the picture, the light falling on what is really there. Crusader/rebel. Story/journalist. Man/woman. He has reduced it all to this: beater/beaten.

I curl into the pillow. If my head does not explode, if I wait another day, perhaps the Polaroid will develop more. We will all morph and form into some new pose. I'll emerge differently, and so will Sam. I'll see him clearly, for once, his character as obvious as his clothes. Are you a good man, Sam? Or are you just a pleasant one?

Jose is outside waiting for his phone to ring. I'm inside waiting for my head to explode. He has done what he was ordered to, and I'm doing what was expected of me. I bleed, I ache, I cry.

The door opens, letting in a wave of heat. Something plastic crinkles as it passes by my feet. He is in the bathroom now; the fan spins on with the light. A tumbling sound then, and I know: ice cubes. The sound of ice cubes going into the ice bucket.

He sits next to me and unknots my bandanna.

He offers ice bundled in two towels. I sit up and take it but don't meet his eyes.

He clears his throat. You realize, he says, if I hadn't done it, my boss—

Yes, I say evenly. I know. Your boss. Sam's clients. Everyone beholden.

200

This is his apology: the dullness of good cop/bad cop. I am disappointed in Jose.

I'll order whatever you like for lunch, he says.

I'm not hungry, I sniff.

Well, it's early yet.

I whip my head toward him. What time is it?

Eleven forty-five.

You bastard, I hiss. He still has fifteen minutes to call you!

He . . . already called.

I blink. *What?*

He called.

Sam wasn't late? That's not what this was about?

No.

He comes over to his bed, sits across from me.

What kind of husband would call too late? he says gently. No man would do that.

I start to cry. Once again, I've assumed the worst. Even a man who hates Sam's politics, despises his greed, wants him stopped at all costs, believes in him more than I do sometimes.

Then what? I say through my tears. Why?

He said he could only get two-thirds of the money.

How much?

Three million. He said he needed to get some from his father on Monday when he's back in town. He said he couldn't send it to the Maquiladora Workers Fund until the next day, and that he couldn't shut down his Mexico office until he spoke to his partners.

You're angry because he needs money from his father?

No. He looks at my swollen eyes. We are angry because his father is not out of town. It is a lie. And . . .

And what?

He keeps saying he didn't do it. That I have the wrong man.

We consider this; our eyes meet but I look away first. The

201

trips, the whispered conversations. Oh, God, Sam, I am not that naïve.

His truthful eyes reach out to mine. Is this a trick? What they did to Patty Hearst? I don't know what to think.

What are Jose's thoughts, his reasons? Sam's? Mine?

There is only what he does. There is only what we all do.

I stayed. I got in the trunk. Sam hedged. And Jose hit me.

North Lake, Antiquing with Ally, 2006

Blue jeans against a red truck, the dark lake in the background. If you look carefully, you can see the edge of the barn, too. The barn where Ally told me I was crazy. She'd told me the same thing at the party with Hugh and Sam: I'd be crazy if I didn't at least meet Sam. Give him a chance. Crazy – as if I didn't know that already.

Dr Kearny's office is decorated better than the others. I should know: I've had nearly as many male doctors as I've had boyfriends. Kilim rugs, terracotta pots. The colours and objects are clues: college abroad. Residency in New Mexico. I look at him and watch him watching me watch his office. Sifting through his life instead of my own. He knows this trick, knows them all.

'I don't feel like talking today,' I say, and he nods.

A minute passes. These are the longest minutes that exist. He waits, knowing this. A staring contest, a waiting contest, any of them I will not win. He is comfortable doing nothing and I'm not. I shift in my chair, move my neck, my fingers. I lick my lips, rub my eyes, sigh yawn sigh. When I can't stand it any longer I speak again.

'Haven't you ever just not felt like talking?'

'Yes.'

'I just, it's just, I mean I don't know if it even helps. If I'll

203

ever . . . improve. It's like two steps forward, one step back.'

'Did you take a step backwards this week?'

I look at his eyes, his kind eyes. It's the only thing the doctors have had in common: these small oceans of kindness, blue green, green brown amber. Float or wade. Stand by the shore. You watch the swirling silt of your own life in them.

Kind eyes but hard questions. Why does he ask when he knows the answer? Why does he always make me say it out loud?

'Saturday,' I begin. 'I drove with my friend Ally up to the lake. There was a really inexpensive cabinet maker there who'd finished a piece of furniture for her. So we took her husband's pick-up truck with some moving blankets and rope and things in the back. We pulled alongside the barn, and a man and two little boys came running out as if they knew us. They were all wearing carpentry aprons. I mean, little boys, maybe six? Seven?

'When we stepped down from the truck, the man looked like he'd seen a ghost. He suddenly shooed the boys away and blocked Ally's path a little. Like he didn't want her to get too close to the barn, you know? And he said the strangest thing.'

'What was that?'

'He said, "We were just building a little birdhouse."'

'And that struck you as odd?'

'Well, part of it was the way he said it: defensively.'

'And then?'

'He brought the dresser out to the pick-up truck and we secured it with the ropes and a few bungee cords. It was a beautiful piece, made of wormy chestnut I think it was, with an inlay for a marble sink. She's going to use it in her master bathroom.'

'Ah,' he says.

'And as we drove away, I couldn't help thinking how they

acted when we arrived. Like they were expecting someone they knew; and once they saw we were strangers, they started making excuses for why the boys were there.'

'And?'

'And I couldn't help thinking that the boys were involved with making the furniture.'

Dr Kearny speaks slowly. 'In that scenario, it would have to be some very talented seven-year-old boys.'

'I know, I know. But . . . dozens of people we know go to places around that lake to get cheap furniture. And this week I made some phone calls to the emergency rooms in that county.'

I lean in, bite my lip. 'In the last year,' I say, 'there have been six children brought in with fingers, or parts of fingers missing.'

I hear him swallow. He nods a little. 'Sawblades?' he says.

'That's what I'm thinking.'

'You may be right.'

'Yes,' I sigh. 'But Ally said I'd lost my mind. And Michael . . .' I shake my head.

'Michael doesn't agree?'

'He said I needed to learn the difference between a lead and a hunch. And between a hunch and a . . .'

'Yes?'

'And a fear.' The last word is a seed between my teeth.

'That hurt you.'

I nod. One tear spills on to my cheek.

'We agreed several weeks ago that Michael is a man very dependent on facts.'

'Six children is a fact.'

'Did he dissuade you from pursuing the story?'

'Practically.'

'But not completely?'

I shake my head.

'So you'll learn more and see if—'

'If I'm right.'

'Yes.'

'You know, I'm right sometimes. Sometimes what I sense, or, or, what I'm afraid of, turns out to be true. I thought David was going to follow me, and he did.'

'Yes,' he agrees.

'Do you have any idea what it's like,' I blurt out, 'never to know anything for certain at the beginning?'

He waits.

'Never to believe, in your bones, 100 per cent, that you are feeling something true? My body . . . it always feels the worst thing first. You know that phrase, "go with your gut"?'

'Yes.'

'If I went with my gut, I'd never leave the house.'

He chuckles.

'It's like the rest of you live in the real world, and I – I live in the fear world.'

'You feel different than other people.'

'Yes.'

'Any other words come to mind?'

I know what he wants me to say, but I don't say separate. I don't say alone. I sigh and say, 'I don't know . . . Kumquat?'

He smiles in spite of himself.

'Time's up, Mrs Kumquat,' he replies.

Saturday is the day they will trade me in. Sam, who asked for Monday, who lied about his father for reasons only he knows, dropped the idea the minute the package arrived. He took one look and changed his mind.

The exact location of the exchange has already been determined – a cabin in the hills. Sam doesn't know this yet: they'll tell him Friday at noon. In exchange for everything he assembles and does, he gets nothing. He gets me.

I know all this now. I know everything, I think: motive, method, reward. I know because beating up a woman makes some men feel guilty. I know because having vodka in a motel room without drinking it is a virtual impossibility.

We are on our third spiked lemonade. Companionably drunk on a Thursday afternoon, discussing ransom and the weather. (Hot.) On the dresser, there are BLTs and potato chips still in a brown bag. I suggested tacos but he laughed at me: American tacos are not tacos, he said. The gallon of lemonade next to it is two-thirds gone. The ice he bought for my cheek is now in plastic glasses.

My head doesn't hurt any more. When I went to the bathroom after the second drink, I saw myself in the mirror. Only one of my eyes was actually black and blue: the other cheek was just reddened, slapped. The first blow, tentative. The second, firm. Bad, but not nearly as bad as David's.

The three-million-dollar punch. For that kind of money,

Sam could assemble a team to replace me: nanny, cook, driver, prostitute. Parts of me are completely worn out anyway. My cheekbones are still high, but the freckles are getting darker, the lines deeper. How much more was I worth at age twenty? I remember Jamie looking at my college graduation picture with a kind of wonder. You used to be so pretty, Mommy, she said.

I don't know how Sam feels about me: I really don't. I only know how he feels about being a family: he likes it. He whistles when we pack sandwiches and set off on a road trip. He smiles on the playground as he pushes two daughters on two chained swings, scissoring his arms. It's just what a man of his age should be. He should have children. He should have a wife. He should not let her die. The minimum: men will always do the minimum.

I'm alone so often, it's possible I have invented Sam. All of it, the sweet moments and the arguments. Lately everything I remember is ugly: doomsday thinking, Dr Mueller called it.

As he tilts the plastic glass of lemonade to get the last sip, ice cubes fall against his face. He doesn't flinch or giggle; he saw it coming. He chews his ice and I watch. His head is swollen, too, I see, with back-up plans, contingencies, variables. It is the way a woman thinks, a mother and wife: prepared for the worst, the landscape of fear. Doomsday squared.

You grew up with sisters, I blurt out.

What? He smiles.

Sisters, you have sisters.

Yes. But what does it matter?

I shrug and drink my lemonade. Jose has a point. He could give me his name, address and phone number and still elude capture. My daughter could find the toffee-coloured crayon and draw his handsome features for the police, and he'd still slip away. I could tell him anything or everything. I could shock him or bring tears to his eyes. Our stories won't change the story to come.

Still, I want to know more than the motive and details of my capture and release. I'm curious and we have some time to kill: it's either talk or get another paper or watch game shows. He fills his glass again: he is not ready to tell me everything. He has not asked again about David. I'll wait.

We talk about Mexico: the deserts up north, the jungles down south. I've only been once, and he frowns when I tell him where: Cabo.

Cabo is not Mexico, he sniffs.

I shrug. He's probably right. The resort where I stayed with my girlfriends was entirely white – walls, furniture, sheets. All I remember is a string of silly bars, drunken Americans holding enormous fish. It was not foreign any more than Disneyland. But on the outskirts of town, there was crushing poverty.

That, he says, is authentic. Some of the biggest slums in the world are in Mexico.

Did you ever . . . live in one?

Practically, he says. My wife and I, before I came up here to work.

Were you illegal?

What do you think?

I don't want to stereotype, I say, and he laughs. You keep offering to order tacos and you don't want to stereotype?

Where else have you been in America?

Florida, he says.

Florida is not America. I smile.

He lifts his drink to mine: the plastic barely clinks.

What is America then? he says after he drinks.

Minneapolis, I reply. Chicago. Maybe Seattle.

Why?

Everything on the edges is cut off from the rest. People in Miami, LA, or New York? They think nowhere else exists.

He nods.

It's only really normal in the middle.

I suppose you are from a state in the middle?

I grew up in Wisconsin. But my father's family has been in Chicago since the turn of the century.

The Great Lakes, he says.

Yes. I smile. My father took me water skiing every Sunday in the summer on his day off.

He spoiled you. He smiles.

Why is it, I ask, that whenever anyone loves someone properly, people say they are spoiling them?

I swallow a throat full of tears, look away.

I'm sorry, he says.

I sniff, nod.

My father . . . has also passed.

I blink up at him. Really?

Yes.

Was he a good man?

He . . . was a principled man.

That's not the same as good.

No. No, it is not.

My parents drank vodka and tonic every Saturday night in the summer, I say, swirling the ice in my glass.

My father drank tequila.

Ah.

I believe he started each day around 11 a.m.

I laugh. Well, it's five o'clock somewhere, I say.

What?

That's what drunks say to each other when they drink at lunch.

Well, then, he says, to five o'clock.

We laugh and clink. He opens the lunch bag. Our BLTs are wrapped in wax paper, like someone's mother made them. They are perfect: summer tomatoes, light toast, lots of mayonnaise. They cheer me back up again. I tell him how, when I went on a diet, I would order LTs, without the B, and if the tomatoes were ripe, you didn't miss the B at all. He tells me about coming to America and having his first hamburger, how bland it was to his fiery tongue. I tell him my children don't even like McDonald's; they want Chinese food, Italian, Thai. It's like going out with a group of girlfriends: they can't decide where to go, argue, negotiate, compromise, then take for ever to order.

So they *are not* spoiled, your children? They are simply loved properly?

I've given this question a great deal of thought. Now I consider it some more, with the benefit of vodka and lemonade.

My husband thinks they're spoiled, but I don't.

He nods. There is a small drop of mayonnaise below his lip. He feels it, licks, smiles.

Sam thinks I give in too much, that they whine and I give in. And you?

I think they're just . . . comfortable expressing their disappointment.

He shakes his head and smiles. A universally male thing: the head shake that says 'women'.

Sam is better with discipline, then?

I shrug. Not really. I think because he's gone so much, they want to please him more. To make their time together happy.

There is a pause in the rhythm of our conversation, and my eyes go up to his.

What?

He smiles. Perhaps there are good elements about your husband being gone.

He roots in the bag and comes up with one wrapped pickle. We could share it, he says.

Is there a knife? I ask.

Why? Do you want to drive it through my heart?

My laugh explodes, bursts through my diaphragm. He joins me, giggling. That boyish high laugh. It is ridiculous, an absurd question. We both know the answer: I do not. That's the problem after all, isn't it? Jose has taken me and hurt me, and I don't want to kill him. I realize later that I believed the worst was over: I have already survived. I have already forgiven. I may be a killer somewhere inside, but I am, apparently, not a killer of him.

I take two bites of the crisp pickle and give the rest to him. He doesn't start eating it from the opposite end, but bites right into my bite, and keeps on going. We wipe our chins with the dispensed white napkins. He puts all the trash, his and mine, back in the bag and takes it somewhere outside. He doesn't flinch when he picks up my greasy papers; doesn't look for a clean white corner to lift.

When he comes back we play Hearts and a few rounds of poker which I lose. We are even, I think. I teach him Kings in the Corner, the game I play with my daughters. I beat him triumphantly, on the first hand, placing the cards around the circle with a snap. Just like math, it all adds up.

He groans with my victory.

He turns on the television to one of those amateur dancing and singing shows. A couple enters and starts to cha-cha.

He looks at me, then leans down to untie my ankles. He stands and holds out his hand in offering.

Let's see if you're as good as you think you are. He smiles.

Oh, I am, I say.

I am drunk but my feet haven't lost their way. We cha-cha in the small space between the beds and the TV, grinding the old shag down even further. He moves easily and quickly, turns me with a kind of knowing. All that tying and untying, the rhythm of it, has seeped into his skin. As the song ends, he dips me on to my bed and lets me fall.

I laugh until the tears appear at the edges of my eyes. The vodka has gone to my head. He stands above me, watching. I could kick him in the gut, between his legs; but he would not be surprised. I am drunker than he is.

I pull my arms into karate-chop pose, frozen, mock-threatening.

Now it's his turn to laugh, and he does.

On separate beds, we watch the last part of the show. The TV glows warm and blue, a summer fire. It dances off the planes of his face, his small ears. I want to watch to see if he sleeps but I can't help myself: I fall asleep on top of the scratchy bedspread, the cheap air conditioner squeaking like a cricket in the room.

When I wake up on Friday, I am re-tied – lightly – and there is a blanket draped over me, folded under my chin once. Military-style.

FRIDAY

Six days. This is usually the point in a journey when I tire of my well-assembled clothes, long for a new brand of shampoo, miss the contours of my own bed. Those longings feel small and decadent to me now.

I wake up and stretch my arms, not my feet. That, I do miss. The lengthening of the leg, the pointed toe, the feeling of being taller than the mattress. When Sam first started travelling, I luxuriated in that stretch and swung my arms and legs to the side, making angels in the snowy cotton sheets. Being alone is fun in the morning. You have the whole bed, the whole pot of tea, the whole sunrise. The dark misery of the night firmly behind you.

I look to my right. He is gone, but my deep sleep each night proves he was here, standing sentinel. Keeping me in is a form of keeping me safe. And I wonder if Sam lay awake on a separate bed, gun in his pocket, if I would feel protected. Is that my problem? Would any man do?

I hop into the bathroom, brush my teeth, wash my face. My clean set of clothes aren't back yet; that's where Jose likely is. I look in the mirror and amuse myself with the vision of hopping through the door, across the parking lot, on to the highway. Just as he turns in with yogurt, muffins, fruit, there I am. His impeccable timing keeps me tied down, not the rope.

Behind me, the key in the lock. I smile at my knowledge of him. Wipe my chin, turn to go.

My heart leaps, falls straight to the floor. I actually hear my own gasp.

It is not Jose. It is not David.

My newest fear is alive in the room. And there is no phone, no scissors, nowhere to run. I back into the bathroom, and this man follows with a grin. He is older, darker, round-cheeked. A dirty kind of Santa. He takes one step forward, I take one step back. My heart is a soundtrack, a pounding instrument beneath my ribs. He can hear it, is that why he smiles? Can he also see my fingers on the sink, scrambling behind my back for my toothbrush with its squared-off dagger of a handle? It skitters to the edge of the sink, falls to the floor.

Your friend will be right back, he says, sitting on my bed. He irons the bedspread with his hand, back and forth, where my chest and shoulders made an indentation. The idea of my warmth on his palm makes me angry.

He's not my friend, I reply, suddenly tough.

He asked me to keep an eye on you.

No, he didn't.

He chuckles, looks around. There is not much to see. Is he wondering if our room is better than his?

Your face doesn't look so bad, he says.

I heal quickly, I reply.

I've pictured an animal in room 9, and he is not quite that. There is no feral grace or speed. He moves deliberately, like there is something heavy and dark inside him.

So you like television? Everyone in America likes television.

There is television in Mexico, I say.

In Mexico the children play outside.

In the next paragraph I will be blamed for fast food, video games, sitcoms, deforestation, oil gluttony, unnecessary wars. Jealousy, greed, anger: they hang in the air, musky, my punishment, my fault. Get in a room with the wrong foreigner, and you really are an army of one. I bite my lip, say nothing.

So . . . what do you think about all this?

All what?

This situation in my country.

What situation?

He leans toward me. *I know he told you. I know you watched the tapes.*

My promise burns, a rim of fire around my pounding heart.

I don't know what you're talking about, I say.

He nods, narrows one eye, considering.

I know this much: I'm a good liar. The lies are always available; the truths are tamped down. Is that why I know nothing?

A car door chimes closed in the parking lot. I hop toward the sound, hop right around him, the lead in my own sack race. He doesn't move an inch. Later, the fact that I did not trouble him, that he did not reach for his gun, bothers me tremendously. What good is a liar who has no power?

I hop to the window, spread the curtain.

You know what I think? he hisses. I think you don't want to leave.

Outside Jose approaches slowly, looking down, laundry in one arm, breakfast in the other. I bang my wrists against the glass. He sprints, parcels dropping, and flings open the door.

Their voices in Spanish fly around the room like something alive. They could be saying anything: chop off her limbs, throw her in the river, watch her sink. Scalp her, scald her, take her clothes off, take pictures. He has the final word, tapping his watch. I hear something that sounds like a number. The other man nods and leaves. In a second, we are alone again.

On his bed, Jose looks different. Something drained from his face. Is it a hangover? Hunger? His eyes have a defeat I've seen at bars, gravesites, losing locker rooms.

I didn't tell him anything, I say.

Good, he says, looking down at his hands.

What's wrong? I say, panic fizzing in my throat.

We are going somewhere else to call your husband at noon.

You mean . . . the two of you?

No. The three of us.

What? Why?

My boss insists.

Has someone seen us here? Are—

No.

I'm a child suddenly. I cannot bear to leave what's mine. My room, room 7. Everything I hated about it has suddenly grown dear. The scratchy bedspread, the narrow curtains, the too-bright orange lamp. The devil you know. His boss is right: I don't want to leave.

I'm not going, I say.

He looks at me kindly, does not say the obvious.

I don't understand, I continue.

You're not supposed to.

He goes outside and retrieves my breakfast. I consider refusing it, indulging in a small act of defiance. If I don't take it, time won't pass. Noon won't come, Sam won't pay, I'll never get home.

One thing has to lead to another. I eat.

We pack.

I have nothing, so it takes him longer. I sit on my bed, he goes under his. I hear him rooting around, fingernails on canvas, plastic. When I lie back and close my eyes I can convince myself he is an animal. A raccoon or bear cub going through trash. The time he takes beneath the bed makes me realize how much is under there. More than the tapes. I should have looked, should have dug, should have taken the time. I had it, after all.

I do the calculations and I'm ready to feel the regret. At first I thought Jose was standing outside, going just to the car, the corner, maybe the front desk. Watching me, the way he had the first day. I imagined the delivery boys: the pizza, the deli, the laundry. The little relationships he had, the howsitgoings, the ties that bind you to a place you are only visiting. The temporary friendliness you can summon. Even me. Those people will have their own awakening, knowing they were part of something criminal. That they helped, in their own small way. And they will say, Oh, I knew it. There was something wrong there, oh boy, oh yeah. One guy and always two meals. It didn't make sense!

But he went to them, I know that now. Got in his car and didn't just move it to a new space or go to the office or dumpster or Coke machine, he left me. Left me with his boss sometimes next door, not always. Trusted the universe for those fifteen or twenty minutes, the ones that I always thought would be three or four, tops. If I'd had a watch or a clock or a true clue about his nature, I would have figured it out earlier. I could have gone. In his own way, he was asking me to. I used to think when Sam travelled, he was daring me to leave, too. You are untethered. Will you stay or go?

In the days before the bars and the deadbolts I could have escaped. The highway wasn't far. When I pictured doing it, in my own romantic way, the running, the hitchhiking, the frantic flagging down, he was always on the corner, pulling up in the Cutlass. A what-do-you-think-you're-doing look on his face. That stopped me, that look.

And how do I explain that to the police? That I was left in a room and didn't leave because I thought Jose was outside and I thought he could see me and that someone was watching and I knew he would shame me, make me feel like a five-year-old with that look that men have? Your father, your husband, your science teacher, the concierge, the policeman.

My puffy eye throbs. If I make it through with just this visible wound, one swollen eye, I'll lie again. I will lie the way women have lied about injuries since the beginning of time. *My kidnapper punished me for running toward the highway, for stabbing him in the thigh with the blunt end of the spoon I should have kept. You should see the other guy.*

Around the room my good eye settles on what I don't want to leave behind. The scratchy bedspread, the orange glazed lamp, the white terry bathmat, thicker than the towel. I love these things suddenly. I have what I have, all the knowledge I can carry, the comforts and memories, the regrets, the shame, the laughs and the dream, that dream. It fills me up. I am packing, too.

When he is done he stands by the door, waiting for me. He has untied my knots and put the rope in his cargo pocket. Jose has done all he can. He watches me as I catalogue the week: the

222

mistakes we've both made, the miscalculations. The wrong time, wrong place, wrong husband of it all. Finally he clears his throat, and I walk to the open door. He takes my wrist not lightly, not tightly. Enough to know he is solidly there. Outside the air is hot and thin. He leads me back to the Cutlass, to where we came from.

As he pulls out of the parking space, another engine starts deeper in the lot. I turn. The other man is behind us in a blue car. The curtains of room 7 are open slightly; his two suitcases sit on the bed.

At least one of us is coming back.

The trees get bigger as we drive: oak, sycamore, weeping willow. Their leaves touch, entangle. When the wind blows they wrestle for space, choking each other, giving oxygen and taking it away. They groan and snap, resisting. The road is an intrusion here, a scar.

Occasionally another car passes in the opposite direction. The models and colours are old: a caramel sedan, a faded blue pick-up. I count them, then stop when it scares me: there are not enough. I ask Jose where we are going and he doesn't answer. Is it possible he doesn't know after all?

I decide not to be scared. I've been abducted, beaten, bargained for. I've survived motel room, car trunk. Being moved is the least of my worries. The real deadline is tomorrow, not today. I repeat these things to myself. I close my eyes, let the trees and cars slip away. The Cutlass seat is soft beneath me again. I'm strapped in, locked in, warm soft safe. Swaddled. The shaking does not come. This is where I am now. I can't picture being home. At the end of a journey, I'm usually making lists for what awaits me. There is plenty at our house that needs attending: skylight repair, alarm system on the second floor, lights on timers, guard dog, curtains, laundry, gardening, mail from well-wishers. No. It is as if I don't live there any more. All I have is room 7. Nothing else matters or exists. That is my personal ransom.

When I open my eyes, the road is narrow and more winding.

We turn on to dirt. My breath catches for just a moment in my throat, aware we have left the paved world. There will be no more BLTs and yogurts, no *Jeopardy*, no Bible, no bed. Now we are camping. Bushwhacking with the animals and trees and sky. If I run I'll get lost. I will not find a stream, a farmhouse or a highway. I'll be eaten by wolves. I don't speak nature any more than I speak Spanish. He knows this, they know this. But my breathing returns. Quickly, it returns.

We are going to that cabin? I ask.

He says nothing.

Was your boss in room 9 all along? I blurt.

No, he says quietly.

Was he in the parking lot?

He turns to me, blinks once and looks back to the road.

The question lay unanswered between us. Does it matter? I wonder. Whether I know if I could have, should have opened the door and hopped away? I didn't, after all. That's all that matters, isn't it, the truth of it. I am not a woman of action after all, Sam. I tried once, got caught, stopped. I accepted that he was smarter than I was, more prepared. His pockets were filled with clever things. He had thought the whole thing through. Counted on me behaving a certain way at a certain time.

And I did not disappoint him.

The gravel is thicker now. A driveway? The small stones fly in the wheel wells, almost festive. Ahead of us the cabin is small, not much bigger than an outhouse. A sleeping hut for loggers, perhaps, if we've travelled north or west, closer to the mountains. If we went south, toward the farmland, I can't explain it. Any further east and I think we would have hit scrub pines, smelled salt, sensed ocean.

I think of the microchips people implant in their pets, GPS systems, homing devices. There are people who have that kind of compass in their heads. They're the ones who can escape into the woods and find their way home. Could Jose have known I wasn't one of them?

We pull up near the unfinished cabin. No phone to pull out of the wall, no running water to fill a bathtub. I wonder about cell phone reception here. He has thought of that surely. I am many steps behind him.

He parks the car and we walk to the cabin. The other man stays in the blue car behind us. When he opens the door, a mouse skitters out, inches from my feet. I suck in my breath and he leads me away wordlessly. I wait by the car as he burrows in the trunk. He spreads a blanket in the flattest part of the field and we sit on it together, breathing in moss and honeysuckle. It's a good place for a picnic, I think. The kind of ground that presents itself to you, a gift. Camp here, sit down, take a load off. We do. I remember the last picnic I had with my daughters: under a tree by the public tennis courts, the plaid blanket, the turkey sandwiches. Julia squishing an ant and Jordan telling her that Daddy told her not to.

I smile and look over at him, about to ask about his last picnic. Something about the furrows in his brow make me change my mind. My half-open mouth closes.

I look at him for a long time, but he stares straight ahead.

I don't like this change in him, the wilderness, the silence. We are in the home stretch and it feels as awkward as the beginning. He is rubbing the tips of his long clean fingers together, rubbing them like worry beads. I look at my own pale fingers, cuticles ragged now, hands bound again at the wrist. If they were free I could reach over and hold his. We could comfort one another in the aftermath, the way wife-beaters console their wives.

The car behind us leaves. I hear the gravel sparks behind me, don't look. I feel his shoulders relax, his breathing deepen. We are alone again.

What's going on here?

We're at the cabin, he says. You were correct.

Why now? Why didn't you just drive here on Sunday?

Shakes his head. Too difficult. No food. We'd have had to build a fire all the time.

Then why, why today? So we wouldn't be followed or—

My boss wanted to place the call from here.

Why?

It's more private.

I think about his words and their careful meaning. Privacy. Alone, further away from the world.

I don't see why we couldn't stay in the room for the call.

His voice is soft and low: Because it isn't soundproof.

I look around at the trees. A squirrel runs up the base of the nearest one, a hawk swoops in the distance. No witnesses. No one to hear me scream.

My swollen eye aches again, the way an old scar fears the scalpel.

His eyes meet mine. There is something close to apology in them. I recognize it: duty.

Your husband . . . still claims he is innocent.

The air is still, but alive. If we called Sam now he would hear the birds and the wind, the low whistle of a train in the distance. Softer than the sound effects of kidnapping: a scream, a gunshot. The crack of a whip before it slices bare skin. And what would we hear in the air where Sam is? The fullness of regret, or righteous indignation?

My teeth threaten to chatter as I speak: What time is it?

He answers without looking at me. Eleven forty-five.

Is your boss coming back for the call?

He looks at me but doesn't answer with language. I see it in his surprised eyes: no. I imagine his boss is guarding the driveway, strategically set up the way I thought all along. The Motorola phone has three-way calling; there is no need for him to be physically present. And if he is not, then I can gesture, communicate. Give him the high sign. If I need to.

There is another way, I say slowly.

What do you mean?

There is something else you can threaten Sam with, instead of my screams.

He raises one eyebrow.

What could be more effective than hearing his wife suffer?

There is a chess-like detachment now; we are speaking of me in the third person.

There is something else he cares about deeply.

He leans in. You have two minutes to explain, he says.

I take a deep breath, as if I'm diving twenty feet. I've never told even part of this story in less than fifty minutes. That's the length of the first visit with a new psychiatrist. The length of a lunch hour with a friend, after we have walked to the restaurant and ordered too much wine. That is how long it has taken to tell. The aftermath is even longer: the friendships that dissolved, the jaws that take for ever to undrop.

I was married before Sam, I say.

He cocks his head. David, he says, and I nod.

I continue: Sam has kept it a secret. He's so image-conscious, his job, his family, his political affiliations. What if he wants to run for office, or be appointed to a post? His parents don't know, and neither do his friends. The country clubs, the Social Register. They ask for documentation of everything. So I changed my maiden name, then took his. No one knows.

Do your children know?

I shake my head.

He shrugs. In America, isn't everyone divorced?

Not from a writer who turned into a drug addict and dealer they're not. David told me he was doing research for a novel, and maybe he was, but . . . anyway, there are more than a few unsavoury ex-boyfriends too.

229

Sam's family wanted a more virtuous bride?

Yes, you could say that.

He nods. It's like that in my country also.

I exhale, relieved.

So that's it? That's the whole story?

Yes, I lie.

He smiles widely, and I wonder if I'm caught.

So . . . these men. These horrible men. These, unsavoury men. Were they white, black or Latino?

I squirm and confess I've never been with a man of colour. Why is he changing the subject?

He laughs at me. You manage to marry a drug dealer, but haven't gotten around to dating anyone who wasn't white?

I laugh a little with him. It seems ridiculous when posed that way.

And why, exactly, would David the drug dealer kidnap your daughter? What makes you think he is capable of such a thing?

I hesitate. My bound hands go instinctively to my necklace, hold the gold rings as if they will keep me afloat. This is not the part I have to tell him; this is not the part he needs to know.

He . . . uh . . . he wanted children. Lots of them, I say. My cheeks heat up and him watching me.

I see, he says.

And I, uh . . . I didn't want to have a family with him. He said if I left him, and had children with someone else, he'd track us down and take them.

He shakes his head slowly. Wow, he says, with just a trace of disbelief.

I can't look at him; my eyes fix on a tree, the outline of leaves.

So that's the tale of David.

Yes, I say. I exhale for what feels like the first time in hours.

That's all?

Yes, I lie. Yes. I don't need to tell him any more.

Well, he was quite a catch.

We laugh loudly; our cheekbones, with their twin injuries, hurt in the same way.

I hope he was handsome, he says finally.

Oh, he was. I smile. They *all* were.

He scratches behind his ear. I don't know, he says. It's not as if you have pictures of Sam dressed in women's clothing.

There is nothing that matters more to Sam than appearances, I say. Nothing.

I don't think you know your husband so well, he says. Even when he's right, you think he's wrong.

I'm right about this, I say. I am.

You have proof?

I nod. There is a blue box in my closet, below a panel. The wedding photos are in there. The paperwork too.

Does Sam know this blue box exists?

Yes.

Does he know where it is hidden?

No.

He pauses, fingers his chin. I see his mind working.

I'll do it on one condition, he says.

What's that?

I'm not going to tell you the condition until tomorrow.

I don't pause.

All right, I say.

Tell me your real last name, he says. Your birth name.

Show me the gun in your pocket, I reply.

He reaches deep inside his left cargo pocket. The revolver is silver and small, innocent as an iPod.

I nod; relieved. I was right to be afraid. Sometimes I *am* right.

Carrington, I say.

He gets up, then stops, considering me.

A drug dealer and an extortionist, he sighs. You have had quite a track record, Claire Carrington.

And that is that. I have traded my reputation for my life. The emotional equivalent of a cut-off ear.

That's what he thinks. I have fooled him in this; perhaps more.

He thinks my shame comes from loving up and down the ladder, slumming in the wrong neighbourhoods, fucking in the backseats of the wrong cars. He doesn't see how wrong he is. How I long to love backwards, back to a place where I'd never notice anything but the dimple in someone's cheek, or the curl of chest hair rising up from a frayed cotton shirt. Sam's hair. Could I not just go back and see his hair? Fall in love with it the way I fell for David's sharp wit and Luke's liquid eyes and Pierre's teacup ears?

One thing. To go back and fall in love with one thing, and extrapolate from there. My old habit, lost now, of assuming the best.

Jamie's First Birthday, 2000

Two shots of her, nearly identical, covered with cake.

Sam had to fly to LA for a client meeting. 'They need me,' he said. 'Jamie won't know the difference.'

'But it's her first birthday. Today is the day.'

His reply: 'There's no calendar in her crib, Claire. We'll celebrate on Sunday when I get back. I'll make balloon animals. I'll do face painting. I'll dress up like a clown if you want me to.'

'Okay,' I sighed, and he kissed Jamie on the head, then me. Hoisted his garment bag and left. A taxi that time. Part of me, the worst part, sank into the sofa, relieved that he would go on her birthday, and not just mine. Business was business no matter who got in the way.

I put Jamie in her high chair, opened the refrigerator and took out the pink cake. She dug into it like a sandbox. Pink frosting in her hair, under nails, down the front of her shirt. Not a Kodak moment. Not the life you remember, but the life you live. When I took the rubble of the cake away, all torso, a carcass of crumbs, she said a single word: 'Again.' I laughed as I carried her to the bathtub, knowing she would have another chance.

He makes the phone call from twenty yards away. He faces me; if I could read lips I would understand every word. As he speaks, a bird caws in the nearest tree. I imagine detectives listening to the call on headphones, trying to discern the bird's origin. North American blackbird. Eats seeds and fruits. Travels in a straight line. I see red pushpins on a US map. Men in short sleeves, Sam in long. He is different than the men trying to help him. They do not need reference books to understand Sam's origin. Wealthy and weak. Educated but not smart enough. The stupid ones always get caught. There I go again. Thinking the worst.

There are two criminals now, only one at large. I've spent nights with them both. We are equals now, Sam and me. White-collar criminal, bad-girl bohemian wife. At last we have something in common. He has earned me now. Is that why he did it? Did he feel us growing further and further apart, left wing right wing, poetry-reading sitcom, political-rally fundraiser, each answering a different call? Did Sam know all along, know he carried a dark spot, a black mark over his heart, looking for a small magnetic match? A small smile creeps across my lips: that Sam actually had it in him. Say whatever you like, but I know this much: you have to be strong to break a law.

He is still talking. He gestures now with one hand, emphatic. It's like watching someone talking in a car: you can sense the tone but not the words. He is firm, unyielding. There. He shakes his head no. There is silence. I see it then, or think I do. At the end of a short sentence. Three syllables, the obvious t-sound at the end. My real maiden name: Carrington.

He nods, says one more word, shuts his phone.

Sam has some explaining to do now. The police could be in his living room, quizzing him. What did he mean? What was that reference?

I'm in a place where everyone knows. The fickle crows, squirrels, raccoon, deer. Nobody mates for life. We need each other for different reasons: to stay warm, to share tasks, to produce offspring, to protect each other from predators who break in through our ceilings.

When Jose comes back the phone is in his pocket. He sits on the blanket and twirls a blade of grass between his long fingers.

Tomorrow? I say.

He nods.

A breeze comes up, lifting the edge of our picnic blanket. I put my foot out to weigh it down. It's calm despite the breeze. We are settled.

I have one question, he says finally.

I turn to him and raise my eyebrows.

Why did you do it?

I, uh . . . knew it would devastate Sam's image. He wants everyone to think he's a certain type of man with a certain type of family.

No, not why did you tell me. Why did you live your life that way? With men who didn't deserve you, like, like . . .

J.Lo?

Yes. He smiles.

I guess I had trouble saying no.

You were taken against your will?

The irony lay between us. He was just one in a long line who had stolen me, swept me away.

236

No. I smile. I went willingly. But I was young.

We were *all* young.

I was still grieving my father. That's what the therapists say. Acting out, choosing badly. I shrug.

You see it differently?

I used to say that anyone worth spending an evening with was worth spending a year with. I could fall in love with someone for the way his hair fell across his cheek. And when I looked at him, that's all I would see.

You are a romantic.

Not any more.

And Sam knew, obviously, about David?

It was part of my allure.

A woman of mystery?

I shake my head, set him straight: I was used merchandise. A bargain. The perfect value for the cheapest wealthy man on earth.

You think too little of yourself, he says.

When I look up I catch something new in the slant of his smile. Ever the writer, I want to name it. Bemusement. Mischief. Blend them together and you end up somewhere surprising. Affection.

Merry Christmas 2005 from Jamie, Julia and Jordan

Three red fleece hooded jackets on a wooden toboggan. At their young ages, a miracle they all smiled at once.

The new babysitter I'm interviewing in the college cafeteria holds the picture up to the light, squinting.

'Two boys and a girl?' she asks.

'All girls.' I smile.

'With boys' names?'

'Well, unisex names.'

She shrugs and I immediately hate her. Want to ask her what the hell she planned to name her children.

'So are you gonna keep trying?' she asks.

'Trying?'

'You know. Trying for a boy?'

I don't hire her, and I don't tell her why.

The cabin is smaller than room 7. It holds two sleeping bags, a cooler, a row of small candles. I'm frightened when he moves to light them: the cabin is made of old lumber. It could all go up in seconds, a structure like this.

Please don't, I say. And he doesn't.

Through the cabin door, fireflies appear and disappear. When I was young, my father told me they were playing hide and seek. We would sit out on the lawn together when he came home late, waiting for cool air, watching their game.

He looks at me looking.

Do you want to sit outside for a while?

But your boss?

He's miles away.

The blanket, folded in a corner, is retrieved. We walk barefoot into the field. The moon is so full I can see bark on the trees. Crickets sing to the frogs. Somewhere above us there is honeysuckle. I breathe in our last night together.

There is something I want to know, I say.

Okay.

Why did you take me instead of Jamie?

Why did you ask to be taken?

They are both fair questions, but Jose is playing with me now. On and off. The fireflies have influenced him.

I want to know, I say.

I thought you'd be better company.

Seriously.

His long breath fills his chest.

My wife, he begins, pauses.

I wait.

My wife was one of the first to die in the Mexican lab. It was the only job she could find. And since your husband . . . well, it seemed equivalent.

I nod and think of the videotapes; she could have been one of the women filmed, toiling away, oblivious.

How long ago?

Nearly two years.

I'm sorry.

I feel his shrug without looking at him.

She was pregnant, he adds softly. Seven months pregnant. We were saving up for the baby.

My own breath catches in my chest.

I was right: he had the face of a father. It was that face that lit up with fury when he described Sam recruiting in the *barrio*. This wasn't about me and my little family. This was about him and his little family. When I look over at him, his gaze is further off, somewhere else. The urge to bring him back is stronger than my fear.

I had a baby with David, I whisper.

I thought if I said it quietly enough, and rarely enough, it might cease to be true. I'd kept it from friends, doctors, colleagues. Now it echoes across the hills. I feel faces in the forest night, turning to me, eyes wide, deciding whether to trust. A woman, another species, who can turn her back on anything.

He looks at me now, blinking, breathing his understanding. At the centre of anyone's heartache, there is always a child.

When? His voice cracks.

Fifteen years ago.

Is he . . .

I shrug, then clear my throat. I don't know.

But, how?

I got this terrific assignment in Paris, I say. After the story I did in Pakistan broke, I got offered a lot of work in Europe. The pay was great and I had a wonderful babysitter back then, so David and I decided to go. But I met this other man researching the story, and – well, David and I had a horrible fight. He destroyed the hotel room. I flew home, took the baby and moved out of his house, a few towns away. The man from Paris – Pierre – came over to visit me the next month. Said he was worried for me. But – David found us. One night when Pierre was out.

And he took the child? he asks gently. David?

A cry rises in my throat, and I nod slowly. He is a kidnapper after all; he knows the end of every sentence is the ransom.

The tears fall and I collect them in my hands. He reaches up to the scar on my right hand, touches it with one finger.

He hurt you? It is half question, half statement.

I raise my head, search his eyes. Was it imprinted on me? Could one man with a gun instantly recognize what another man could do?

Maybe it will help to tell me, he says.

I wipe my tears. He came in through my bedroom window, I say softly. When I saw the gun, I . . .

He waits, I swallow and breathe.

I ran to the crib, grabbed the baby, I whispered. Not even two years old . . .

And then?

I made a mistake, I sob.

We all make mistakes, Claire.

I look up at the sky, then at him. No one, I choke out, has made as many mistakes as I have.

Tell me.

I didn't run, I say. That's what I should have done. Taken him and *run*.

What did you do?

I held the baby in front of me, like a, like a shield.

I put my head in my hands, as if I could suffocate myself with it.

David loved him, I say. He hated me, but he loved him! And I didn't think, I never thought, I sob.

You never thought he'd shoot his own son?

I shake my head violently. I grab for the rings on my necklace, counting them like the rings on a tree. Four gold baby rings.

Claire, I—

I was holding him like this, I say. I lift my hands to demonstrate.

My right hand was wrapped around his legs. The bullet hit my hand, and then his leg, and—

And you dropped him.

I don't need to say yes, don't need to nod or cry out in agreement. My choking sobs are his answer.

David ran out the door with him, bleeding from his leg. I don't know, I say thickly, if he is dead or alive. If he walks with a limp, or is paralyzed—

Didn't you try to find him?

Yes. Oh yes, But the police . . . they seemed incompetent. I always thought they'd end up leading him to me, instead of the other way around. I still use a private investigator, but I've heard nothing. In years, nothing.

The fireflies blink on and off, briefly illuminating a tree or section of grass. The green of summer, even at night.

That's why it worked, he said.

What?

Your bargaining chip. Sam couldn't risk that it would get out, that David would find you and the girls. It wasn't about his parents or appearances at all.

No. Are you angry with me?

He puts his arm around my shoulder and I lean in to the space between his chin and his chest. We are side to side, touching, even our feet. His left against my right. I feel the smooth brown toes, clean and even, not the feet of a criminal, the feet of a paramedic who has lost his wife and child.

We stay like that a long time, edge to edge, staring off into the darkness, two people peering into the night as if what they have lost can be seen in its deep shadows.

I'm sorry, he says finally.

It's not your fault, I whisper back. It's mine. All mine.

SATURDAY

In the morning, there are granola bars, boxes of raisins and water bottles spread on the blanket. He apologizes for the lack of tea; we cannot risk building a fire. Not yet.

It's early; the birds are loud. We take turns going to the bathroom in the clearing. We finish the food, sit on the blanket. He pulls the deck of cards from his cargo pocket and we play Kings in the Corner, Hearts, Spit. We take turns losing, take turns pretending to care. We're polite and delicate with each other. The way people are at a funeral, avoiding the inevitable goodbye.

After cards, I show him how to make a daisy chain. He whistles through a blade of grass. Aren't we clever, we think as we smile to each other. But what next? There are trees we could climb, limbs we could swing from. We could walk through the woods while I named each plant and leaf, the Latin word and the English, the edible and the poisonous. We could find a divining rod and go where it leads us: to water, to shelter, to other, away. We could, we could.

I haven't thought of lightning striking, brush fires, gunfights, fisticuffs. My eye is healing and perhaps so is my brain. Did Jose knock some sense into me?

I ask about the logistics of the money going to the foundation, imagining a suitcase or paper bag. He skims the surface of an explanation: an electronic transfer, the non-profit account in Mexico. I think of how technology has changed kidnapping: MapQuest, Google, online banking, three-way calling. But some things never change: gag, blindfold, handcuffs, telephone. Those are the basics, Kidnapping for Dummies.

He looks at his watch.

We have a little over an hour, he says. What do you want to do?

Ice skate, I answer.

He laughs. And after that?

See a movie. Read a magazine. And you?

I would like to fish. He smiles.

We could ice fish, then ice skate.

Yes.

We settle in on the blanket and speak of the places we can't go. He tells me fishing stories, deep sea and surf, bonefish, sailfish, mackerel, trips with his friends in Mexico. He tells me the tourists don't know where the fish are. He tells me more about fishing than Sam ever has.

I tell him about the ice skating lessons Ally told Sam to give me when I turned forty, the smoothness of the ice, the Olympic joy when I first learned to spin.

He looks at his watch again. I have something you could read, He says.

What?

He goes back in the cabin and comes out with a bundle of mail. The *Sentinel*. Two catalogues. A phone bill. A small FedEx box.

I look at the labels, the dates. My name, Sam's.

When did you get these?

He shrugs.

The paper is dated the Saturday before. The mail I was too lazy to collect. I scan it for anything important: terrorist activity, suburban rapists, child molestations. In the lower corner of page six, there is a two-inch square: *Child Labor Probe in North*

Lake. I suck in my breath. There it is: children, furniture, family factories. OSHA representatives investigating. I think of Michael reading it: realizing he'd been scooped. That I was right, and he was wrong. I smile.

I scan the catalogues: one cookware, one home fabrics. What comes when you renovate.

Why don't you open the package? he says.

It's addressed to Sam.

He raises an eyebrow.

I look at him, a man who would pry open another man's skylight. What is a package after all?

I pull the tab on the envelope: a blue Tiffany box falls out. I pick it up off the blanket and hold it in my palm.

Open it, he says.

It's probably a joke gift, I say. Once Sam put a red plastic Monopoly house in a box with a note that said, 'Smile. I'll be home soon.'

Open it.

I lift the lid. Inside is a curved mesh bangle. I blink, close it, look at him.

Maybe Sam is having an affair?

Perhaps, he says carefully, it's your birthday present.

It's a month away.

Yes.

I shake my head. He could have a girlfriend in another state, I say.

Well, I hope it isn't his secretary, he says. She's a bitch and a half.

I laugh loudly.

What?

That phrase. You're starting to sound American.

God help me.

He takes the paper from me and folds a section into a triangular hat, puts it on my head.

251

Smile, Jose says. You'll be home soon.

He steps off the blanket, walks twenty feet away. He makes the call from a second cell phone in his pocket. I hear him but don't hear him. The directions, the instructions, the tone of voice different than the way he speaks to me.

Wait, I cry out.

He turns, touches his hand to the mouthpiece, covering it.

Tell Sam, I say firmly, that you won't give me back unless he can tell you what colour my eyes are. And what I take in my tea.

He blinks at the foolish woman on the blanket, fingering her new bracelet, hoping it was meant for her.

I look up at the sky, pale blue with a few thin clouds, too diffuse, too scattered to hold a silver lining. This is all I want, after all. These are my demands, what I've been searching for: to be *known*. To be loved the way I have loved. For the beautiful details.

He turns his back to me and I don't know what he says. If he ignores me, if he asks, if Sam answers properly. But a few minutes later, when he comes back to the blanket he tells me it is time to go.

Jose gathers up the things in the cabin. A few he puts in a back-pack: matches, flashlight, rope, water. I don't know what's already in there, only what he puts in. He takes me outside, points to the woods.

A hundred yards in, there is a rock about four feet wide, he says. That's where you will wait.

A rock, I say.

There is a plastic bag with water, food, a blanket and a compass.

I shiver.

You won't need any of them. It's just a precaution.

Okay.

I'm going to take you there, then double back and torch the cabin before I leave. I don't want you to be afraid when you see the fire.

But someone will see the smoke.

Yes.

Then how will you—

Don't worry about me. It's time to worry about yourself now.

The word, my word: worry. Now it's time to worry. I've been given permission. The rest, the dozen years, were only practice.

We walk to the woods. It's still damp underfoot from last week's rain. Each step releases pine and sage.

The rock is flat and wide as a loveseat. I put my hand against it; cold. The plastic bag of supplies is propped against one side, as he said.

We stand there for a minute.

What did Sam say? I ask, finally.

Sam?

About my eye colour?

He blinks twice, gathers himself.

He said . . . that your eyes change colour depending on what is near you. Like . . . a blue dress. A stormy sky. The pale green of the Indian Ocean.

Tears come to my multi-hued eyes. I see the photos, remember each in the box. The blue Easter dress with the full skirt, the grey clouds in the California mountains, the snorkelling boat in a green cove off Perth.

You have seen it, I say. You have it. The box.

Yes, he answers. My, uh, boss went through the master bedroom pretty thoroughly.

He was there too? When?

Later that night.

My girls, I say. Oh, God.

They were asleep. He was in your room only. We were interested in Sam's bureau.

How do you know?

I know, he says too quickly.

I nod, wipe my tears.

So you knew everything already? Everything I told you?

No. I just . . . looked at some of the pictures. So I knew exactly what Sam meant.

I don't know if he is telling me the truth. About that, or anything. And why do I expect him to today when I didn't earlier in the week? He is tripping over his words now, his rhythm is off, the way Sam's is when the girls ask how long he's going to be gone. Not long, he says. Back before you know it. A lie tumbled with kindness until it comes out pretty.

He takes my hand, presses a key into it. Room 7, it says on the plastic green tab.

The box is under my bed, he says. Put the key in your pocket and don't tell anyone you have it or where we were, or they'll get to it first. Remember I said I'd tell Sam about it under one condition?

I nod.

Here is my condition: tell your daughters.

Tell them what?

Tell them everything.

I shake my head. They'll hate me. They'll think I'm weak. They will think I'll leave them one day too.

You have to tell them the truth, he says.

I finger the key, can't meet his eyes. What is the truth?

That you had to leave. That you had to leave and search for the right man to be their father.

I blink. You think Sam is the right man?

He's a good father, isn't he?

He says it almost angrily, then moves a few paces away and picks up kindling at the base of a tree. The twigs fill his hands quickly, and he curls up his shirt to hold them. He doesn't speak. What could Sam have possibly said in those hushed conversations that turned Jose into his poetic defender? What did he see from his observation post? What clues did I give him?

Did Sam really say that about my eyes? I call out.

Yes, he says.

I put the bracelet on my wrist. It is wide enough to cover the raw scrapes from the ropes.

And, he adds, he said your youngest daughter's eyes are exactly the same shade.

I smile. And what did he say I took in my tea?

Uh . . .

255

I look into his dark eyes, unchanging, where the truth is pooling, waiting.

He had a little trouble with that one, he says.

And there it is: our last laugh.

He re-ties my hands and feet. The knots are softer than before, looser, like the new bracelet. I think if I rub them against the rock, I can undo them. Erosion over time.

He is about to go. He is not going to wait for laundry, or fetch me breakfast. We have shared our last meal together and I don't even remember it.

I look over at the cabin, imagine it aflame.

I don't see how you will be able to escape, I say.

He smiles. I have that car with the excellent tyres, he answers.

We smile but don't laugh, as if we are trying not to wake the birds in the trees. When my face settles down again, there are tears pooling in my eyes.

I'm afraid to be alone, I say.

The truth spills out when I'm with him. Things I took years to learn or say.

He looks at me, nods. He knows this. He knows it all. He is my last doctor. He has all the notes, all the careful recordings.

There is perhaps one other option, he says quietly.

I could go with you? I say hopefully. Half kidding. But if half is kidding, the other half is not.

This is what I've done, all these years. Left one man for another. Run away. Never alone.

I breathe in and out. I have children waiting for me and policemen coming for me, I say to myself. The aloneness is temporary.

Well, he says. I could stay and make sure—

Blindfold me, I say suddenly.

What?

I can say that I was blindfolded the entire time, that I barely saw you in the dark that night.

He blinks.

That way I can't give them a description of you. They won't expect one, won't try to wear me down.

No.

Why not? I was blindfolded in the Polaroid. It makes sense.

He shakes his head. What if something goes wrong out here, what if you need—

I'll be okay.

You can't move, you can't see – what if you have one of your panic attacks?

I'll survive, I say. And I believe it.

He tears a three-inch strip off the bottom of his T-shirt and wraps it around my eyes. It still smells of soap, the last room 7 shower he took. Soap. Dust. Redwood. I will never walk into a motel room without thinking of him again.

He guides me gently by the wrist to the rock.

You'll hear me going, he says. And you'll hear when they come for you. It shouldn't take long. Even out here in—

Mid-County? I say.

I'll hear the guns clanging in their holsters, SWAT team equipment jangling on their backs. It will be different, far different than the sound of Jose walking away.

I hear him swallowing, deeply, next to me.

Thank you for the blindfold idea, he says. I'm . . . sorry I had to hurt you. And.

He pauses. There is a third thing in the list.

I give it to him: I'll miss you, Jose.

Tears fall beneath my blindfold.

I hear his hug coming, a slow swoop, arms soaring softly,

and then he is around me. My hands are tied but I lean my head into the soft curve between his shoulder and neck. His cheek and chin are soft, as if he had shaved for me. I either feel or imagine I feel his lips brush against my hair.

He stands back, lets me go. His thumbs are a shadow over my eyes, soaring in to wipe away the tears on my cheek. Then I hear a sound my father used to make: both palms against his eyes, wiping away his own.

When he steps away the air is cooler.

It takes all the strength I have not to call out to him, to say what I think.

Don't leave me.

He stands there a minute watching; I hear his deep breath.

You won't be alone for long, Claire. He says. Not any more.

It takes a few minutes to unfold and reveal, this final gift.

Sam will not be travelling now.

He has given me my husband back.

I'm not the only one in my house who has bad dreams. My daughters have them often. They aren't tortured, as I am, by the vivid details: silver knife, cold green eyes, wall of orange flame. No. They come to me tear-stained and sweating, afraid of the bigger picture, the characters and plot lines: a man was chasing me. A dog was biting me. I was falling.

On Sunday, before I opened the mail, before the skylight broke open, Julia called my name. She'd been to my empty room and back to hers, stood in the doorway sobbing. Not knowing I was downstairs packing my briefcase at this impossible hour.

What is it? I asked softly from the stairs, as if I didn't know. I hugged her and lifted her back into bed, told her to think of good things, like ice cream. Like soft puffy clouds. Not poison. Not thunder. Not boots on stairs, whips cracking the air. No. Not those things.

I lay in her bed and held her for a while, didn't say what I wanted to say: *I'm scared too. I hate the rain. Daddy always leaves us. I dreamed a man with greasy hair and electric eyes was choking me.*

She was nearly asleep when she said it, but I was wide awake when I replied.

Don't leave me, Mommy. *Stay.*

Okay, I whisper.

A promise to pile on the others until they all break. I hope she forgets it the way she will forget the dream in the morning. The morning she woke up and Mommy was gone. Really gone.

I hear squawking, rustling. I picture squirrels sniffing near the flat rock, deer and rabbit watching from a cluster of trees. A few minutes later, I hear the whoosh of flames from the accelerant. I imagine I feel its heat. Do I?

I wonder how orange the fire is, how wide, how tall. If it burns away the trail that led from his life to mine.

I close my eyes beneath my blindfold, give in. Beneath my eyelids I don't see my fear, don't see my veins throbbing or limbs shaking. I see Jose and his boss in the Cutlass, driving back through Mid-County, heading south. The whole length of the journey I imagine Jose sitting in my seat.

I hear helicopters above me. I crane my neck upwards, instinctively. Had he factored those in?

They hover above the field, but don't come closer. They are watching, a whirling metal lookout.

Later, when the SWAT team approaches, they call my name. As if they have no intention of taking the wrong bound and blindfolded and bruised woman.

I turn in the direction of their noise, but don't speak. Let them think I'm gagged, doped, traumatized. They undo the ropes roughly: thick fingers, calluses, nails. It hurts more to be untied than it did to be tied. They are unschooled, unclean. He's worth ten of you, I want to shout, but don't. As always I overlook the concretely true: they were smart enough to find me.

They bombard me with questions I don't answer. I act like I'm in shock, and I am. Not from being in the forest, not from being lost, but from being found by these brutes, these men who talk and don't listen, who bring in helicopters when they need hunting dogs.

I endure a few hours in their company: notetakers, sketchers, hunch followers. They give me water, pretzels, soda. They give me pressure and silence. I have little to say. I don't answer their questions successfully –*Where did he take you? I don't know, I was blindfolded* – and they don't answer many of mine.

Have you found him?

Where is he?

How is he?

You tell us, one of them chuckles.

I glare. Do not correct. Let them think the worst.

They give up and sigh, looking at me as if I'm just a broken machine they have to work overtime to fix.

We're trying to help you here, one of them says.

Well, you could be a little nicer about it, I say. A little more charming.

Charming? he said, eyes wide.

I think of Sam when I say this. Sam, whose whitewash of charm was offered instead of money, knowledge, wit. Sam, who remembered jokes but forgot birthdays. Sam who tickled the girls with one hand while he deftly removed their Band-aids with the other.

A little charm goes a long way, I reply.

Before they escort me home, a desk clerk gives me a towel and lets me wash up in the precinct bathroom. My face in the mirror is tougher, still bruised, but not older. Like a boxer, I think. I wet the white towel and hold it to my face.

The letters scratch against my cheek and I pull it away.

Mid-County Police Department, it says.

The patrol car takes me out of Mid-County, back down my street, my block, my driveway. The construction dust is gone. The dusky light warms the stone walls. The flowers, the bushes and shrubs are lush, satiated. They have been watered. Did Sam pay someone to come?

We pull up in front of my house. The window boxes are trimmed, the steps have been swept, and the garbage is tucked away. I've never seen it so clean.

When the patrolman opens the car door, Sam steps outside. He is smiling, but looks tired. I smell of sweat and mud and moss; I expect him to put one arm around me, but not too tightly. But he grows long and tall, uses both arms, pulls me in. He clutches me even as the known world slips away, and brushes his lips across my swollen cheek.

A few minutes later, when we stand apart from one another, I notice how clean he looks, how his hair shines in the sun. He runs one hand through it, boyishly, the way he always has, but his fingers touch grey strands here and there, ones I never noticed before.

I open my mouth to speak, to ask him a million questions, but they don't come out. I am tired, suddenly. Deeply tired.

You need some sleep, he says.

I nod.

As he opens the door I hear my daughters' bare feet running above me. A sound I will never tire of, whether they are running down a grassy hill, across an elementary school stage, or through the concourse of an airport after a semester abroad. The sound of coming back.

It's over now.

Yes, I yawn.

No, really, Claire, he whispers. We found David.

What?

Remember that window guy who thought he knew you, Roger? He worked for David last year. Turns out he'd seen your picture in his house.

But what about—

Sam shook his head. David's not talking. But there's hope, Claire. There's real hope.

I tried to feel the hope, the lightness of it in the room, in the seconds before my daughters tumbled into my arms. But there wasn't time. Just as there wasn't time to consider whether Sam was wrong or right; if he had been right all along.

March 1991

At the bottom of the box is perhaps the most beautiful photo I have ever taken. Everything about it is right: the colours are lively, the expressions are joyous. It is impossible to look at it and think the worst.

The sky is blue. The wagon David is pulling is red. And the fifteen-month-old boy sitting inside it is blond. His hazel eyes, which David considered his, and I thought were my father's, are shining. The look on my son's face is gleeful. Pull it faster, Daddy, more more more. His chubby fingers, mid-clap, are slightly blurred. This tiny imperfection is what centres the photo. What makes it worthy of framing. When I look at it each year on his birthday, I am grateful that he is not looking at me, not reaching for me. He loved his father, I say to myself.

And then there are all the things you cannot see. The bruises on my wrist as I hold the camera. The empty phials in the garbage can after one of David's rampages. And on the other side of the wagon, hidden, are the curly yellow letters I painted myself.

Jesse, they say.

As usual, I cannot sleep. I'm not afraid, though; I'm restless. Everyone is tucked in, tired and happy, deep into their dreams. Not me.

Sam cooked an expensive dinner. Alaskan salmon. My favourite. A splurge for him under any circumstances, let alone our current bankrupt state. The girls wouldn't let me out of their sight. Sat on the bathroom floor while I took a shower. I don't know when I'll be able to take a bath again.

I walk downstairs for a drink of water, and when I come back up, I stop.

The skylight stands tall above the landing. Sam has checked it and fixed it, he told me proudly. The same way he worked tirelessly with the police, watered the plants and swept the walk. A new Sam, with time on his hands. Guilty, worried. Not tan. I expected him darker, somehow, more dangerous, like the men who personal-train edges into their silhouettes. But no, he was so pale he looked almost fragile. As if he'd been stripped to his boyish essence. Or, I realize with a start, just pale in comparison to Jose.

I sit on the last step and look up. I see no stars, no light, nothing.

In the end, you could say that Jose was sick. That he was vengeful, violent. You could say that a man who was willing to steal a child was the lowest form of human being. But that would be worst-case-scenario thinking. Because you could also say this: he chose me. He listened to me. He knew me. Those were the kind of details I could have fallen in love with once. I still wonder what detail of mine made him drop Jamie's wrist and take mine. I like to think it was something Sam could love too: my slightly crooked front tooth. My uneven dimples.

Or maybe, just maybe, he felt my furious desperation. That I would not let another man take another child away from me. Never, no, never again. That was why I went. But then, there were all the reasons I stayed.

I lay down on the landing. The Berber carpet is scratchy beneath my skin, like the bedspread in room 7.

I think of the compartment in my closet that used to hold the box, and now holds the motel key. Tomorrow I'll go there to claim what's mine. I'll take a screwdriver and remove the deadbolt, the extra chain lock. It could all go in a velvet pouch with the twine from around my wrist. Those will be my mementos now. On the way back I'll get a BLT and an iced tea to go. I'll pick up a newspaper, do the crossword, and look for news of Jose the way I used to look for news of David and Jesse. If they have found him, if there is a picture for me, a caption, the last puzzle piece I need: his name. It could be a new syllable, light and easy, filled with vowels. At night I will roll it around on my tongue, imagine saying it, my awkward accent, the turn of his head, the flash of his small white teeth. I'll walk to the window and know he is out there; know that he always was.

I stand up and walk toward my bed, then stop. A small sigh from Jordan's room, followed by a deep breath. As if she is diving under the sea. I fix her covers, smooth her blonde hair, kiss her damp forehead. I move on to Julia's, then Jamie's. It seems I've been travelling in a circle between them, bed to bed, butterfly kiss to butterfly kiss, for all of my life. What did I do before when I couldn't sleep? Where did I pace? When I walked around the block, through my small apartment, the piles of my own clothes, the nothing of my life, was I in the same flight path, always, just circling above them, waiting to land? And Jesse, my sweet Jesse. If he was alive, was he too big, too angry, too hurt to be tucked in?

I know Jamie is awake the moment I step in her room. Her breath is softer than it is when she sleeps.

Hi, honey, I say.

I can't sleep, she replies. I keep hearing things.

I don't ask what kind of things, don't tell her they are nothing, don't suggest she cover her ears with a pillow. We are beyond that now. I give her the facts. Daddy checked the skylight. Daddy installed a new alarm. You can sleep in our room if you want.

Mommy? she asks, as if I'm not there, as if I could be someone else.

Yes?

Remember before I could read, you and Daddy told me bedtime stories?

I smile in the dark, remembering. Sam started this: He would ask the girls to give us two characters each, and he would meld them into a story. Jamie always asked for the same two things: a princess and a mean fox.

I like reading at night, she says, but sometimes I still want a story.

I swallow hard before I agree, trying not to let my voice break. Tomorrow, I say. I'll tell you a story tomorrow. I turn on her bathroom light and close the door. She's asleep before I hit the hallway.

Frame up, windows in, 2007

Everyone takes a photo of this stage. It's as ghostly as an ultrasound: each room shows its bones and eyes, no more. In the kitchen, you can only imagine the pale painted cabinets, the green glass tile, the silver rocket-ship appliances. For now it appears to be all windows, letting the outside in.

Upstairs in the master bedroom, three casement windows face the backyard. No iron bars, no bulletproof glass, no fresh white caulk that comes off on a finger. No. But look closely, beyond what the photo can reveal, and you sense one pane of glass that is not quite flush. A level would find it; a foreman might; a policeman would not. The lenses of hindsight: whoever installed it from the inside removed it from the outside. And entered easily, as often as he liked or needed, without requiring a walk on a slippery tin roof.

And who could know the significance of the lengthening shadow on the lawn below, as the last of the hired Mexican installers stood and watched me snap the picture, lingered just a moment, before moving to his rented truck?

So many things he noticed, collected or changed without us seeing him.

All, except Jamie. She knew she'd seen him before. Walking below her mother's windows, in broad daylight.

The door to room 7 opens easily, laughably so. I could have kicked it in, I think. How many times could I have kicked it in? So many things I got wrong, so wrong. I step on to the carpet and stand in the dark, surrounded by colours I know by heart: orange, green, red wood.

The drive took less than ninety minutes. I found Mid-County with no trouble, unencumbered by rope, blood, worry. When I rolled down my window to take the turnpike ticket, the wind was warm but soft. Vacation air. I pulled my Land Cruiser into the Cutlass's parking space. The Motor Inn's office was dark, and so was the red vacancy sign.

I flip the wall switch but it doesn't work. The crack in the curtain is wider now, letting in a bit more light. His bed is not as smooth as it was before; the bedspread is caught on one side of the frame. I straighten it with my hand, then move around the bed to turn on the orange glazed lamp. It's brighter than I remember; the light travels up and spreads across the sparkly ceiling. Everything pale-coloured around me gives off a painful glow: the plastic ice bucket, the towels in the bathroom, the small slippery soaps.

I sit on Jose's bed and breathe deeply. It smells as clean as it is bright; I sense the final slivers of an ivory bar melting in the bathtub drain, as if he took one last quick shower. I smile, thinking of his dark wet ringlets. No. Impossible.

I look at the windows, the large one in front, the small one in the bathroom. The extra glass, the iron bars, are gone with their fingerprints. The window installer took them away as easily as he brought them in. The room that hasn't changed in years has managed to change in just days.

I crouch between the door and bed and lift the nubby bed-spread. The familiar smell of dusty carpet is there, but not the quilted container. The box sits in its place, small compared to the pressed indentation on the green shag. I pull it out, and behind it, something darker than the carpet catches my eye. A tape. One of the tapes from Jose's bag.

I pick it up, hold it flat in my hand, testing its heft. No number written on this one. I don't hesitate long; I put it in the box with my things. My knees creak as I stand. After I turn off the lamp, I open the nightstand drawer to make sure the Bible is still there for whoever comes next.

Ah yes, the Bible and the remote. What more could the next traveller need?

I sit outside for a few minutes in my car, watching for signs of life, of someone coming or going in the middle of the night. The truckers, the salesmen, the people who get up early to bake bread or bundle newspapers. No one comes, no one goes. What has changed? I try to picture Jose in another motel room in another city, not sleeping. Getting up and walking outside, leaning against a new car, drinking coffee from a new cup. A different kind of same. Did he think of me as he signed the guest register and ordered just one beverage, one meal? Did he think about the truths he told or the small and necessary lies?

The quarter moon above me is pale green, so bright it's almost pulsing. *Tell the gentleman in room 7 I'm looking at the moon. Is he looking at the moon?* I think he would like that story about Sam and me calling each other. I can imagine his voice: *Your husband is not without redeeming qualities.* Defending him even as he took his money and his wife. I smile in the parking lot. Now that is the definition of charm, isn't it, Sam?

I put my car in reverse, and head home.

The house is quiet except for the slight hum of the air conditioner. I hang up my car keys and go to the den. I pull out the sliding shelf with the old VCR and wipe a layer of construction dust off with my hand. The tape is old too; it moves with a plasticy squeak that carries the picture from blurry to clear and back again. Almost telling us a story, letting some of the pieces in, but not enough. I imagine my daughters' faces as I struggle to explain the characters: a stolen brother. A country's women in danger. And what of the others? Are we heroes or charming villains?

On the screen, the camera pulls back further and further in the makeshift factory, until an auburn-haired man appears just at the right edge of the frame. He does not run his hand through his floppy hair. Does not smile his loopy smile. Because when you look carefully, when you do all your homework, when you are certain you are right and not wrong, you see he isn't Sam. He is Hugh, Sam's partner. Heavier by perhaps ten pounds. Taller by an inch. I move my good hand across my face. That's what took Sam so long to gather the ransom: the conversation, the negotiation he must have had with Hugh. Hugh begging for loyalty; to keep Anne and his kids out of it. Not a meeting with his father that Monday, but Hugh. The tape is at the end, stretched, about to break. Hugh turns to his right, and nods his head. Talking to someone only partly in frame. I see an arm, a blue blazer, a white cuff. It could be anyone. It could be Sam. Yes. Maybe. In it together, perhaps? The other tapes, if I had them, might tell me more. Sam might tell me everything tomorrow, or he might lie. The box of photos at my feet shows all of my life; every flash of pain, every beginning, every clue. But this is in motion; slippery. It shows nothing. Proves nothing. Nothing at all.

The tape stops, but not the tapes in my head. Those could loop around for ever if I let them. They spin with the blend of love and doubt that turns to obsession. Sam is or isn't innocent. Jesse is or isn't alive. I could stay and keep digging. I could leave with my daughters, one toothbrush and one set of clothes. I could live in a motel room or a cabin and not come back unless I have an answer. I am strong enough, perhaps, to do this. But is this the strong thing to do?

I turn off the machine and walk to the hall closet, open it. Sam's suit bag hangs there, next to my rolling luggage. They are from the same set, bought at the same time, but his has faded to almost grey; the sturdy black weave of mine is still shiny. I finger the airport tag still stuck to his handle: SFO. Not Baja, not Mexico City. San Francisco. The last place he went.

Back in the den, I sit alone on the suede sofa where it all began, and start to open the mail. Later, years later, when I sit on different chairs and tell the tale again and again, as my daughters and their daughters drift toward sleep, they may feel the point of the story more deeply, its wicked implications. What it makes me. Who I released and who I held tight. I let go of my son, but held on to my husband and daughters. How to account for this?

There is a thud upstairs. I don't jump; I hold the sharp letter opener in one hand, securely, and walk slowly into the hallway, my head tilted upwards, toward the unbroken skylight.

I don't know, after all, what breaking it sounds like. I don't know the difference between a storm and a squirrel and a window snapping out. Between a construction worker and a kidnapper. A husband and an extortionist.

But I know more than I did last week. I know the importance of small things, of clean clothes, a bath, fireflies. I know the relief of sharing secrets. And I know a man doesn't do yard work and grill salmon on the same day unless someone he loves is due home.

And I know this: this sound, the one I hear now above me, is nothing to be afraid of. My fingers relax around the weapon in my hand. This sound is my family walking in the hallway. The creak of floor muffled by carpet. I can almost hear the knuckles rubbing sleep from eyes. Someone is up. Someone is tired. Someone needs something, but I don't know who it is, or where it might be. In this house of mine, so carefully transformed, I don't know what anything is. And I may never know, ever, even as Sam tries to walk me through every room, cradling me close as he once did his baby daughter, telling me the name, the new name, of everything we have left.

Acknowledgements

I am grateful for the unflagging support of my husband, my children and my sister. I thank the brave Dorian Karchmar and her wonderful colleagues at William Morris, and all the fine people at John Murray for shepherding and polishing the project to such a high gloss.

And lastly, thanks to my father for driving me to the library every Saturday of my young life. (And to my mother, who probably told him to.)

Read on with Kelly Simmons online

There's lots more on Kelly Simmons' website and blog,

bykellysimmons.com

You'll find videos and interview podcasts, plus essays and rants about the publishing industry (her favourite topic).

And if you sign up for her free newsletter, you'll be the first to get news, fiction and essays penned by Kelly every other month.

**Check out bykellysimmons.com . . .
and happy reading.**